Every Witch Way but Omens

Magical Misfits Mysteries - book 9

K.E. O'Connor

K.E. O'Connor Books

EVERY WITCH WAY BUT OMENS

Copyright © 2023 by K.E. O'Connor

ISBN: 978-1-915378-58-3

Written by: K.E. O'Connor

Chapter 1

Weird and windy

"Don't let it go! If this thing gets its claws through the bars, I'll lose an arm." My wonderful witch, Zandra Crypt, had her most powerful restraint spell wrapped around the middle of a giant spine-backed belching toad. Sparks of her iridescent magical flames licked around the creature, not to injure it, but as a warning that it should stop fighting us. We weren't its enemy.

The warty-skinned creature writhed and hissed inside the cage, moss green fumes shooting from its leathery mouth.

"I won't let it touch you." I had an equally impressive spell wrapped around the beast as I hurried along behind them, preventing it from lifting its powerful front limbs and slamming them into Zandra.

We'd been hunting the toad for days and were three hours into overtime when we'd finally trapped it in a cage that we'd baited with lavender candy and sour grapes.

The foul tempered toad hadn't been amused to discover its chaotic adventures were at an end. So far, the creature had torched five award-winning landscaped gardens in the area, a wildlife preservation, and Crimson Cove's public park. It was only a matter of time before someone got in its way and it killed them.

Zandra continued along the corridor in animal control, heading to the back rooms where we kept pens that housed captures and rehabs. "Barney! We've got a live one here. We could do with a hand."

Barney popped his head out of his office. Tiredness sat beneath his eyes in puffy purple sacks, and his hair, what was left of it, looked like he'd been raking his fingers through it. "We're full! Glenda and Randal just got back from visiting Poppleton Lodge. The place was surrounded by six miniature griffins looking for a fight. They got them all."

"What are we supposed to do with this?" I jabbed a paw at the writhing bundle of green fury. "It almost set light to a school bus full of children that got in its way."

The furrows on Barney's forehead deepened as he inspected the struggling creature. "Why are all the magical creatures behaving so strangely? In all the years I've worked here, I've never seen anything like this."

"We can figure that out later," I said. "We need to put this thing behind bars. And then my witch needs a break."

"I'm good." The gravelly tone in Zandra's voice revealed the lie in those words.

"Sorry, sorry. Of course. I'll find somewhere to put it." Barney hurried out of his office. "I have emergency pens in the sheds out back. Can you hold it for another five minutes while I put one together?"

I nodded, and Barney dashed away. I was bone weary from using so much magic, worried about the deep cut on my witch's forehead, and my stomach growled almost as loudly as the toad. It had been hours since I'd had a decent meal, surviving on speedy snacks before tackling our next batch of misbehaving critters.

Thumping and cursing came from the room containing the pens, suggesting Glenda Ridgeback and Randal Nix also had a battle on their hands.

I checked my restraining spell was secure so the toad wouldn't escape then slid over to Zandra and leaned against her calf. "I know I've occasionally commented that our job is less than exciting, but I take it back. Give me the paperwork and the routine visits any day over this."

The toad snarled as if I'd said something offensive to it, so I pulsed soothing magic over its leathery form.

Zandra leaned against the wall, her face sweaty and her shoulders down. "It's been a weird few weeks. Ever since the Blood Moon Festival, Crimson Cove has felt different. On edge. And the animals sense it too."

"I'm not sure Remus's festival has anything to do with it," I said. "He holds the same event every year, and there are no records of bad behavior following previous festivals."

She looked down at me, her head tilted to one side, her dark hair sticking to her neck. "You're thinking the gremlin symbols popping up everywhere are causing the animals' frustrations?"

"And everyone else's. That's a more likely connection than the vampires celebrating an ancient rite. Those symbols are multiplying, and we still don't know who's putting them around town." Ever since we'd discovered the gremlin chaos cult symbols in Oak Park Ridge, everything had slid out of control. It started with more calls to animal control about misbehaving critters. Then the weather turned freezing, and fierce winds relentlessly whipped through the town. It should be a balmy summer evening out there, but we'd been fighting hailstorms and the occasional tornado while working.

And then there were the residents. Angel Force had pulled in extra staff from outside the town to deal with the fighting, lawbreaking, and chaos causing. Crimson Cove no longer felt safe.

"If we had more than five minutes to spare, we could research those symbols in more detail," Zandra said. "But by the time we get finished here, all I have the energy to do is shower, eat, and sleep. Then we're back on the job."

"We need to find the time," I said. "If those gremlins and their symbols are the cause of our problems, things will only get worse if we don't tackle them."

"Have you had any success convincing Cythera she needs to make the symbols a priority?" Zandra said.

I grimaced and twitched my whiskers. "The last time I talked to her, she shut the door in my face. She's even surlier than usual."

"And run off her feet, since magic users are misbehaving as much as the animals. I heard from Finn the cells have been bursting all week."

"Cythera needs to understand that, if we don't tackle the cause and only treat the symptoms by handing out fines and sending people to court, there'll never be a solution." I flicked a globule of toad slime off one paw. "Crimson Cove will turn into one of those darkly chaotic magic towns everyone gossips about but no one visits. Even I'm thinking it's time to leave if we can't fix this."

"Juno! It's not like you to give up when there's a twisty challenge facing you," Zandra said.

"I'm not thinking about me. I'm worried about you. That's the second time in a week you've taken a whack to the head."

Zandra gently touched the bloody bump on her forehead. "I'm made of tough stuff."

"You still need to rest and recover."

"At the moment, it feels like we'll only rest when we're dead."

"Don't put that worrying thought out there, or we're definitely moving."

She grinned. "You'll never give up on this place. You love Crimson Cove as much as I do. We've built a life here. You have friends here."

I sighed. Zandra was right, but I had to put my witch first. Every time we stepped out the door, whether it was to tackle a feisty animal or get takeout, we put our lives at risk. Either there was a bolt of lightning striking the ground, a surly neighbor wanting to start a fight, or an animal rampaging, looking for someone to bite.

Barney reappeared at the end of the corridor, looking red-faced. "The pen is ready."

Zandra pushed away from the wall, and we moved the grumpy toad into an already crowded containment room. The air was alive with hisses, growls, and grunts. There was also a potent mix of pungent, eye-watering fear farts drifting in the air.

And there wasn't an empty cage to be seen. Every type of magical creature you could imagine had been misbehaving, centering their misdeeds on Crimson Cove. There was a blue-beaked eagle that had tried to blow up the town hall. A hybrid sloth-snake with wings that littered the road with unfertilized eggs that exploded when touched. And then there was the thorny rodent pup that covered one street in toxic sludge that people got stuck to when they walked on it.

Glenda looked up from the other side of the room, a bandage held in one hand. "Hey! You both lived to fight another day."

"It was touch and go. What happened?" Zandra walked over, concern on her face when she saw Randal holding a bloody towel against his side.

I stayed with the toad, ensuring it didn't make any sudden moves, but I was always keenly interested in any interaction my witch had with her potential beau.

"Randal got bit by a baby basilisk." Glenda hissed air through her teeth. "I thought I'd lost him when the thing dragged him into the sea and tossed him in the air like a piece of candy."

"Basilisk! I thought you were sent to deal with griffins?" Zandra inspected Randal's injury.

"That was the first case of the day. We dumped the griffins and then got a call about some sea creature trying to take people off the beach." Glenda rolled her eyes, swiping a hand over her tight jeans. "We got there and were looking around when the thing grabbed Randal."

"How did you escape?" I asked.

Randal opened his mouth, but Glenda beat him to it. "I was considering whether to dive in and act like the big heroine when this shower of sparks shot out of the water. I did a double-take when I saw Randal was suspended in them! He was flying around like an angel."

"You used one of your gadgets?" Zandra lifted a hand to touch his swollen cheek but then stepped back, a flush of warmth spreading across her face.

His cheeks matched hers and became a charming shade of pink. "It was just something I've been working on in my spare time. How are you? Your head looks bad. You should get that injury checked in case you've got a concussion."

"It's better than your bite wound. Make sure he gets healed," Zandra said to Glenda.

Glenda smirked. "You can treat him if you like. We'd use the same potion. And you probably have a more tender touch."

Zandra glanced at the grumbling toad. "No can do. Duty calls. Maybe check in on you later?"

Randal nodded. "I'd like that."

"You'll be lucky. There are three more jobs waiting for us once I get Randal back on his feet. Open up and take your potion then we're outta here." Glenda pinched Randal's nose and forced a healing potion down his throat. She had no tolerance for weakness in others and expected everyone to live up to her feisty werewolf standards.

Zandra kept one hand raised as she joined me, ensuring her spell restrained the toad, and flipped open the pen door Barney had left in the room. She backed away, keeping a safe distance from the creature, and stood beside me as we floated the unfortunate beast into the pen. Barney had left water, food, and soft bedding inside, so it would realize no harm would come to it.

But there was no point in trying to reason with it. I'd given up on doing that with any of the enraged creatures we'd recently encountered. Whatever you said to them, all they wanted to do was rampage and destroy. And we'd be failing in our jobs if we permitted that.

Zandra secured the pen door and stepped away. "Mission accomplished."

I looked at the shaking pens and angry animals, the fear adrenaline flowing through the air making me jittery. "Let's hope everyone's on their best behavior tomorrow when our next shift starts since there's no room here for any new arrivals."

She rolled her shoulders. "We need to tackle those gremlin symbols ASAP, don't we?"

"We do. But we need to fix that head wound first then you need to clean yourself up so we can go to the inn."

She raised her eyebrows as we nodded goodbye to Glenda and Randal and headed along the corridor. "We're still going to that?"

"I'm curious to see what's been done to the old place. It's sat empty ever since we moved here."

Zandra stifled a yawn. "I am too, but I just want my bed. And food. And to not stink like a gassy bog toad spat at me."

I nodded. I wouldn't push my witch to go to Lila Mingler-Mist's preview party for her new boutique guest inn. Zandra's recovery and happiness were the most important things to me. "We'll send our apologies and go another time. Lila will understand."

"She's most likely postponed her preview party, anyway. With the bad weather and even badder behaving residents, now's a terrible time to open your doors to show off all the money you've spent. A group of grumpy locals would probably push their way in and trash the place for fun."

I'd have flicked my tail in agreement, but it had yet to grow back, so I settled for another nod.

Five minutes later, and after I'd healed Zandra's injury, we said goodbye to Barney and finally headed home. A fierce wind raced along the streets, knocking over waste containers and garden ornaments as we hurried along.

"It feels like the seasons have gotten flipped around." Zandra tugged up the collar of her black jacket and shivered.

Thunder rumbled overhead, and a crackle of lightning briefly lit the gloomy late evening.

"It looks like a storm is setting in. Third one this week." I dashed along beside Zandra, glad to climb the front porch of Vorana Stowell's house and our home.

We made it two steps inside the front door before there was a shriek, and something hit the floor with a clang.

"That was your fault!" Vorana's tone was worryingly shrill. "Why are you always hanging around me? I'll trip over you and break my neck if I'm not careful."

Zandra raised her eyebrows and looked at me. "Who's she arguing with?"

I sped into the kitchen to find Vorana glaring down at Sage, her elderly familiar. "Is something wrong?"

Vorana's angry green gaze flicked to me, and she sighed. Her typically warm smile was absent, and rather than her usual pleasant scent of ink and paper, I got a slug of rancid rage. "Where have you been?"

"We had to work overtime. Same as the last few nights." Zandra appeared behind me. "What's up?"

Concern bubbled inside me as I studied Sage. Her hackles were up, and her chest heaved in and out. This fight must have been going on for some time to make her so agitated.

"You could have told me you'd be home so late. I've been worried. I thought something had eaten you or torn you to shreds and used your bones as toothpicks. Someone said there'd been a dragon sighting, and it would be just the stupidly heroic thing you'd do, chase down such a creature." Vorana tossed a dishcloth into the sink. "All I do around here is worry about other people and cook for them. What kind of life is that?"

"A life of kindness. And we're always grateful for your wonderful cooking," I said cautiously, not wishing to inflame Vorana's fury.

There was a movement on a kitchen chair. Ember Dreamscape watched the explosive scene with a smug expression on his adorable, kitten face. Sage had been unable to get rid of him, and he was a permanent fixture in the house. Much to her disgust.

"Move out of my way." Vorana hissed at Sage, flapping her hands. "Every time I turn around, you're there. You're so needy."

"Sage is supposed to be wherever you are," I said. "She's your most loyal familiar. She loves you."

"If she loved me, she'd give me space. I can't breathe. There's always someone wanting a piece of me. I never have time for myself." Vorana stomped to the other side of the kitchen and yanked open a cabinet door.

Sage hung her head. "Sorry. I know I'm not as fast as I used to be. I'll be better."

Vorana glanced over her shoulder and rolled her eyes.

A thump against the kitchen window made me jump. Zandra's ghoul mother, Adrienne, and her boyfriend, Joel, had their faces pressed to the glass.

"Help!" Adrienne said.

Zandra raced to the back door and pulled it open. Within the blink of an eye, Adrienne and Joel were there, their arms outstretched, teeth snapping, and ghoul eyes glazed.

I lunged in front of my witch, my heart in my throat, and zapped them with a knockback spell before they touched her and contaminated her with a bite.

"Sorry!" Adrienne staggered back, one hand covering her snapping teeth. "We need help. We want to attack people. All I can think about is eating brains. It's disgusting, but it also makes me drool."

"Uh-oh. The weirdness has gotten to you, too." I zapped them again to make sure they didn't get closer. Even though Adrienne was the most sentient and evolved ghoul I'd ever met, if she bit anyone, it would still be fatal.

"We're out of control." Adrienne's eyes were full of unshed tears. "We chased Cannibal Bill for two hours trying to eat him. Please, lock us up."

"You're that bad?" Worry etched lines into Zandra's face, and I could see she was torn between hugging her mother and obliterating her.

Adrienne nodded and then snarled. "Stop us before it's too late. We don't want to hurt anyone. I couldn't live with myself if I turned anyone into a ghoul."

Joel lumbered toward us, snarling and snapping, and got a stinging spell to the groin from my murder mittens that put him on his knees.

"Vorana, I need to lock them in your concrete shed," Zandra said. "Anything in there you don't want damaged?"

She sighed dramatically and crossed her arms over her chest. "More hassle! All you do is make demands and expect things from me. What do I get in return?"

"Not bitten by a ghoul?" I said. "The shed key. We need it."

That sharp comment earned me another grating sigh, weighted down by a world-weariness I'd never heard from Vorana. "Do what you like. Just keep those things out of my house. I don't want any gray body parts dropping on my newly cleaned floors."

"You have snow chains in there, right?" Zandra held out a hand for the key.

"If you break them, you buy me new ones." Vorana slapped a large key into Zandra's palm.

With some effort and a number of knockback spells I could ill afford to dish out, we got Adrienne and Joel inside Vorana's shed. It wasn't a pretty shed with glass windows and cute curtains, but a hulking chunk of concrete and steel, just perfect to imprison two bite-focused ghouls.

Adrienne repeatedly snarled and snapped and then apologized as Zandra hurriedly wrapped them in chains while I twirled a restraining spell around them.

"It's okay. We know why this is happening to you," Zandra said as she edged the metal door shut. "You'll be back to your old self soon."

Adrienne jangled a chained arm. "I hope so. If not, you'll need to put us out of our misery. We can't live like this."

"It won't come to that," I said. "Stay strong and try not to eat anyone."

Zandra closed, bolted, and locked the door. Then we applied a powerful spell around the shed to ensure they couldn't break out if they felt in the mood for fresh brains.

She closed her eyes and massaged her forehead. "This is serious. That sneaky gremlin magic is messing with my family. We tackle it now."

"Agreed. We'll grab dinner from Vorana and then figure out a plan of attack."

More thunder rumbled overhead, and the gloomy cloud-laden sky was briefly lit with jagged shapes as lightning ricocheted around us, charging the air with a static buzz of energy.

We dashed into the kitchen to discover Vorana still scowling and Sage looking like the most defeated familiar ever to trudge around this town.

"We thought we'd eat in tonight," Zandra said. "Something simple would be perfect. And quick."

"I thought we were all going to the opening of the new inn," Vorana said. "I was looking forward to a night off from slaving in the kitchen for ungrateful tenants who never say thank you."

"The inn will have to wait," I said. "We know what's behind the problems in town. And we could do with your help—"

"You expect me to cook for you again?" Vorana jammed her hands on her hips. "All I do is cook, clean, and chase around after you. You're like the children I didn't realize I'd given birth to. You always expect there to be food on tap. I've had enough!"

"You always say you love cooking for us," Zandra said.

"I lied. I'm sick of it. I'm sick of you two as well. I want you out of here. Pack your stuff and go. You've got until the end of the week, but then I want my basement back."

"Vorana! You don't mean that." Sage trundled over on her harness. "You've been so happy since Zandra and Juno moved in."

"I'm not happy." Vorana turned her back to us and filled the sink with water. "Just go."

I hopped onto Zandra's shoulder and pressed my booping snooter into her ear. "There's a free buffet at the inn, and hopefully, no one there will yell at us. Let's escape while we can."

Zandra winced as lightning flashed outside. "Are you sure you want to risk it?"

"I'd rather face a thunderstorm than Vorana in a foul mood," I whispered.

Sage gestured for us to go, a dogged look on her fluffy cat face.

Zandra nodded and tiptoed away until Vorana's muttered cursing was muffled, and we crept outside.

Chapter 2
Inn-teresting times

"It must be the gremlin chaos magic affecting her." I balanced on Zandra's shoulder as she hurried through the freezing evening, tiny slivers of ice raining down on us like frozen needles.

Zandra sighed. "We've just been evicted."

"No, we haven't! Vorana will come around. It's this weird magic. It's making people behave out of character. Your mother is the sweetest ghoul I've ever known, but she just tried to take a chunk out of your arm. And Sage is never one to back down from a fight, but she seemed broken. And I've never seen Vorana and Sage argue. They're always adorable together."

"What about us?" Zandra rested a hand against my side. "What if this magic affects us too, and we start hating each other?"

"Do you have any feelings of loathing for me?"

"No! Never. I still think you're as frustratingly adorable as ever."

"And I feel the same about you. If I get any vengeful desires to do anything hateful to you,

I'll let you know before I cast the first lethal destruction spell at your head."

She chuckled. "Likewise. Let's get inside before we're blown off our feet or zapped by a bolt of lightning."

I clung to Zandra's shoulder as she dashed past houses and stores. Crimson Cove was eerily quiet. It was just past eight in the evening, but there was nobody outside. Perhaps they sensed trouble in the air. And it wasn't just the weather acting up. I had to narrow my eyes to see it, but odd magic sparked around us. Tiny flickers of red and green in the air that tasted of smoke and stagnant pond water.

"Wait for me! I'm sorry. I didn't mean any of what I yelled at you."

Zandra slowed. She turned, and there was Vorana running toward us. She had Ember snuggled in his usual papoose wrapped around her middle, and Sage in her arms, her harness still attached, as if Vorana had grabbed her in a hurry.

"I don't know what happened to me. I don't want you to move out. I love you living with us." Vorana wheezed out a breath as she slowed. "I just saw red! This hot rage slammed into my stomach, and I got so angry. You were right in front of me, so you got the brunt of my rage."

Zandra let out a gentle sigh. "That's good to hear. Not the hot rage bit. That sucks. But I'm glad we won't be homeless at the end of the week."

"Never! I didn't mean a word of it. I just... I don't know. I felt out of control. I'm so sorry. Please forgive me." There were tears in Vorana's eyes.

"There's nothing to forgive," I said. "Nobody is acting like themselves at the moment. And I was going to ask if you'd help us figure out the reason why, so we can stop it."

Vorana blinked. "Of course. But what is it that's making me so mean?"

"Let's go to the inn. We can talk more in there," I said. "But you're right. We rely on you too much, so you deserve the night off. Lila is providing a buffet, so there'll be plenty of food."

"It won't be as good as mine. It'll be cheap, processed store-bought muck that's full of sugar and food dyes you can't pronounce." Vorana clamped a hand over her mouth and then lowered it. "I've been in such a foul mood. One second, I'm fine, and the next I want to batter people with books. And I've been rude to so many customers this week."

Zandra slung an arm around her shoulders and gave her a squeeze. "I'm sure they were just as rude back. There's something in the air that's making people testy."

"Something rancid that needs to be blown away," I said. "Although we'll get blown away if we stay outside."

"Or zapped by lightning," Sage said. "My fur is standing on end because there's so much static electricity in the air. And something else. Can you feel it?"

I nodded. Crimson Cove felt on the edge of a deadly, toxic blade of magic. And when that blade plunged down, I wanted my witch nowhere near it.

"Juno's right. Let's go to the inn, and we can talk," Zandra said. "Figure out a solution to your rage problem and what else is troubling the town."

Vorana pressed her lips together, looking like she was fighting not to argue with us. "Yes. Let's do that. But pinch me if I get nasty. I don't know what's coming out of my mouth until it's too late. Then I feel guilty."

"I'll get Juno to swipe you with a paw if you get too rude."

Friends back together, we hurried to the end of the street, turned right, took the next left, and discovered the warm, welcoming glow of the Whispering Willow Inn in front of us at the end of a long street.

"I'm intrigued to meet Lila," Vorana said. "Everyone's been talking about what she's been doing, but nobody knows much about her."

"I've seen her coming and going," Zandra said. "She said hello a few times, but she's always busy and not had the time to talk."

"Builders have been working on the inside for weeks," I said.

"I didn't even know anyone had bought the old place," Vorana said. "It's been empty for almost two years. It belonged to the same family for decades before that, but the son wasn't interested in keeping the business going, so he closed it and moved away."

As the witches gossiped about the inn, I studied the building. It was a delightfully wonky three-story construction with a pitched roof and small windows. Ivy crept up part of the walls, casting a green hue across the freshly whitewashed exterior. The front door was a massive wooden creation, with intricate carvings of crows, wolves, and owls. A new sign had been stuck to the front.

"I heard Sorcha and Gaian are coming tonight," Zandra said.

Vorana chewed on her bottom lip. "They are? I haven't seen Sorcha for weeks."

Vorana and Sorcha Creer had had words after the chaos of the Blood Moon Festival. None of those words had been pretty, and they hadn't spoken since.

"This could be a chance to extend the olive branch," I said. "Sorcha must be missing both of you. And she must be tired of that bore she's saddled herself with."

"They seem as tight as ever. I tried to go into the café one afternoon, but one of Gaian's shady gang members stopped me. He said I'd been blacklisted! And I heard a rumor Sorcha banned all vampires from her café." Vorana shook her head. "What's she thinking?"

"That's terrible news for the local vampires," Zandra said. "Sorcha's always looked after them."

"It sounds as if Gaian is making her suppress her natural connection to vampires," I said. "I understand he has issues with them after everything that happened between him and Remus, but it's cruel to deny a magical being her birthright."

"If Sorcha comes tonight, I'm not sure what I'll say to her." Vorana lowered her gaze. "Maybe too much has happened between us, and the friendship is lost forever."

"Not your friendship. You two are perfect for each other," Zandra said. "We just need to get Sorcha away from Gaian long enough so she realizes what a controlling dweeb he is, and she ditches his fake leather-clad behind."

We reached the front of the inn. Zandra pulled open the door, almost losing her hold on it as a gust of wind blasted into us. We staggered into a pleasantly warm hallway lit with softly hissing wall sconces. The scent of old books and burning candles filled my booping snooter. A large fire crackled in a grand hearth in a nearby room, sending out warmth and light. And although I appreciated the inviting interior, there was something in the atmosphere that had my hackles lifting involuntarily.

"Hello! Is there anyone here?" Vorana said.

A few seconds later, footsteps hurried toward us, and a short, petite woman with a mass of curly blonde hair appeared. She was approximately thirty, with a round face, wearing a smart blue dress. "Hello! Are you here for my reveal party?"

"We're not too late, are we?" Zandra said. "I'm Zandra Crypt, and this is my familiar, Juno."

"Greetings," I said. "You have a beautiful inn."

"Thanks. You're not late. You're my first visitors."

"Maybe the bad weather is keeping people away," Vorana said. "I'm Vorana Stowell. I own the local bookstore. And this is my familiar, Sage. And Ember. He's a new member of the family."

Lila smiled and nodded at everyone. "I'm glad you came. I was thinking no one wanted the inn to reopen when no one showed up."

"Your business is all residents have been talking about," I said. "We always welcome new people into the town."

"I've been worried locals wouldn't approve. I know I've caused a mess with my builders coming and going. I asked them to keep the noise down, but when you're knocking down walls and fitting bathrooms, things get noisy." Lila played with a chunky green pendant on a silver chain around her neck. "You're sure people like my inn?"

"They'll adore it," I said.

She peered out of the window and frowned. "I didn't expect such terrible weather. I figured the middle of the year would be the perfect time to open. I'd get some late summer guests and test things, so I'd be ready for a busy vacation season. Is it always like this in Crimson Cove?"

"The opposite," I said. "It's a pleasant little town, and we usually have weather witches on hand to stop bad weather from ruining planned events. Things have just been odd recently."

"You can say that again. When I first came to look at the place, the area felt safe. Plus, the sale price was amazing. I couldn't believe I got such a deal. It was almost too good to be true. Now, I'm wondering if it was." Lila smoothed the velvet curtains at the window.

"You have nothing to concern yourself with," I said. "Perhaps you could show us around? Then we can recommend the inn to others when we see how amazing it is."

A smile lit Lila's face, revealing slightly pointed teeth. "I'd love to. I'm proud of my first business. I want it to be a success."

The door behind us crashed open, and Cythera and Finn staggered in, their wings rumpled and their usually neat white uniforms creased and blotted with mud.

Lila's expression brightened. "More visitors! I'm so glad you could make it."

Cythera smoothed her wings back into place. She looked around the group, her piercing blue eyes narrowing as they settled on me. "We can't stay long."

"Still problems with the townsfolk?" I asked.

She arched an eyebrow but said nothing.

"We're still having problems at animal control," I went on. "It's something I'd like to talk to you about whilst you're here."

Cythera shook her head. "You're not still going on about those ridiculous symbols, are you?"

"What's this?" Lila said, her attention on me. "Do you also work at Angel Force?"

I addressed Lila. "You won't be aware, but my wonderful witch and I often help the angels with their most troubling cases. When they're stuck with a twisty mystery, they come calling."

"You make us sound incompetent," Cythera snapped. "I handled things fine before you showed up, throwing your weight around and proving to everyone you were something special."

I twitched my whiskers. "I have nothing to prove in that field."

"Not now," Zandra whispered. "We need the angels on side with this gremlin issue."

I held my tongue and settled for sternly glaring at the grumpy angel.

"Nice to see you again." Finn stepped forward, a smile on his handsome face as he shook Lila's hand. "This place looks amazing. I've been looking forward to our visit all day."

"We're not staying long," Cythera repeated. "We have too much work to do."

"Of course! But please, let me show you around. Then we can eat." Lila stepped to the side. "Shall we start with the bedrooms? They're not all finished, but I have two ready for guests."

"That sounds perfect." I remained on Zandra's shoulder as we followed Lila to the bottom of a set of dark wooden stairs.

The front door blasted open again, and Sorcha and Gaian appeared. Gaian was dressed in his usual fake black leather pants and shirt, with a long cape down to his knees. He had a large scuffed satchel over one shoulder. Sorcha was also dressed in black. The color did nothing for her pale complexion and made her beautiful ginger hair look dull.

"We're not too late, are we?" Sorcha's smile faltered when she saw us, and she looked at Gaian.

"No! I was just starting a tour. Welcome!" Lila hurried over and introduced herself. "Do you know everyone here?"

"Unfortunately," Gaian muttered. "We just dropped in to say hello and to welcome you to Crimson Cove. Most of us are friendly. Of course, there are always a few bad apples. I can tell you who to swerve."

"The nerve of the man," Vorana muttered.

"You must stay for the tour. And the food!" Lila said. "I have too much."

"I love meeting other business owners." Sorcha checked in with Gaian again. "We can stay, can't we?"

Gaian sighed softly. "Of course. Not long, though. We have things to do."

Finn walked over, easing the tense atmosphere as he greeted Sorcha and Gaian. "I've been excited to have a snoop all week. Looks like Lila's done something special here."

Lila blushed and lowered her gaze, no doubt charmed by Finn's angel grace and sparkling good looks. "I was glad you could make it. Both of you."

"It's important we welcome new faces to the town," Cythera said, "and ensure they understand the laws they must abide by if they're to stay."

"Oh! Of course. I filed the relevant paperwork, and I have my insurance to hand. You can see it if you like." Lila turned away.

"There's no need. This is simply a friendly social call," Finn said. "As Cythera said, we're here to welcome you and let you know we're close by if ever you need us. Although, I'm hoping that won't be the case. Crimson Cove is a peaceful place."

"I thought so when I first visited," Lila said. "Although, since the weather got so wild, I'm wondering what I've stepped into. And a few days ago, I saw a group of warlocks fighting. They were throwing spells like rocks. One of them got knocked out."

"That was just high spirits. Probably a bachelor party. How about that tour?" Finn glanced at Cythera, but her impassive expression gave away nothing to reveal how serious the warlock fight had been. From the outbreaks of violence I'd witnessed, it wouldn't have been a gentle shove around for jokes.

While they chatted more about the inn, I kept watch on Sorcha. She hadn't once glanced at Zandra or Vorana. She'd remained glued to Gaian's side, one hand tucked around his elbow. There was a frosty air between the witches. One I intended to thaw once I'd removed Gaian from the equation.

A bang from overhead in an upstairs room made me tense. "You must have a window open. You need to get that closed before it blows off its hinges."

"Everything is shut. I made sure of that when the wind picked up," Lila said. "That was probably Willow. She's the inn's resident ghost. Willow's been here a long time. I even named the place after her."

The lights flickered as if confirming that surprising statement.

"Don't worry. Willow is sweet. And the way the lights are malfunctioning, she'll be here any second so you can meet her," Lila said.

"You knew the inn was haunted before you bought it?" Finn asked.

"Not exactly, but I sensed something unusual. I have no issue with ghosts, though. So long as they're friendly, I'll be friendly back. Although I wondered if that was why I got the inn for such a good price. Not everyone wants a free spirit roaming around and scaring guests."

The temperature notched down several degrees, and the wispy figure of a dark-haired woman in her early twenties wearing a long, plain dark dress appeared. Her intense gaze was anxious as it flicked around the group.

"There's nothing to worry about." Lila walked over to her. "Remember, I told you we were having the preview party tonight? These are some of our guests. Make sure you welcome them."

Willow continued to look uneasy but nodded, giving a half curtsy as she did so.

"Greetings. How long has this been your home?" I asked.

"A long time." Willow's voice was a warbling wobble of a whisper.

"She's shy around new people," Lila said. "Willow told me she was trapped here by a hex."

"That's terrible," Vorana said. "Who did that to you?"

Willow lowered her head. "A bad person. I took something I shouldn't, and I got caught."

"And trapped forever?" I asked. "That's a harsh punishment for such a simple crime."

"Crimes must always be punished." Cythera fluttered her wings.

"By being trapped in one place for eternity? That's harsh, even by your exacting standards." I flicked an ear at Cythera.

She ignored me and checked her watch.

"We get along fine, don't we?" Lila said to Willow.

Willow nodded, drifting gently on the air currents.

"Why doesn't everyone grab a plate of food?" Lila gestured to the food-laden table in the nearby dining room. "Then you can eat while you walk around. I'm just about bursting with excitement to see what you think of the place."

I didn't need telling twice, since I'd been starving for hours. I nudged Zandra into action, so we were the first to arrive at the buffet table, shortly followed by Sorcha and Gaian.

Gaian's critical eye roamed over the food. "I'm disappointed to see plenty of animals have been sacrificed for this gluttonous spread."

I rolled my eyes, glad when Zandra didn't respond as she filled her plate with mini sausage rolls, meat sandwiches, and several slices of delicious looking smoked salmon, which I assumed were for me.

Once everyone had their food, Lila took the lead and led us up the stairs. "I kept the theme of the inn traditional. The original style was based on classic European Gothic architecture. The Europeans build such stunning structures, so I didn't want to lose the inn's character by whipping everything out and making it modern and bright."

"I'm glad you did that," Vorana said. "It makes me sad when these old buildings lose their quirks."

"Exactly! I'm new to the hotel business, though, so I was worried about getting things wrong." Lila showed us several bedrooms that needed to be painted and furnished. "I needed a change, though. My family wanted me to stay home and marry a boring guy from my village. But I've always wanted more. This is my way of proving myself to them."

There were eight bedrooms on this floor, all with their own bathrooms. Only two were finished, although there was no carpeting on any of the floors. As beautiful as wooden floorboards could be, they were chilly on the toe beans.

"What did you do before opening this inn?" I asked.

"This and that. I couldn't stick to anything. My parents were despairing of me and pushing for me to settle into a life of dull domestic drudgery, so I tried something different. I took a risk and grabbed this place when it came on the market." Lila flashed me a nervous grin. "Don't tell anyone else, but I'm terrified. I have to get this right."

Vorana patted her arm. "You're doing a great job. And I'll mention the inn to anyone who comes into the bookstore and asks about accommodation."

"Thanks. That would be wonderful. I'm not booking in guests yet, but it won't be long."

We headed back down the stairs, and I felt much more relaxed with a belly full of smoked salmon. We inspected the guest sitting room, and Lila was about to take us into the kitchen when there was a hurried thump on the front door.

Lila dashed to the door and opened it. An elderly man and a woman with a mop of bedraggled gray curls fell inside. The woman's face was streaked with blood.

Chapter 3

Surprise arrivals

The man clutched the woman's arm as blood ran down the side of her wrinkled face, soaking into the collar of her white blouse. "Please, help me. A flying rock hit my wife."

"Come in, come in." Lila caught hold of the woman's other arm and assisted them inside.

Zandra rushed over with Vorana, while I clung to Zandra's shoulder, almost shaken off because of her hasty movement. Between the three of them, they got the couple away from the growing storm and sat the old woman in a chair.

"I'll get a cloth to clean you up." Lila looked around the group. "Is anyone good with healing magic?"

"We've got this." Zandra crouched beside the woman, inspecting her head wound. "Hey, I'm Zandra. This is my familiar, Juno."

"Mrs. Simister. Gwendolyn." The woman's cheeks were blanched of color.

"That cut looks nasty, but it isn't deep. How do you feel? Any headaches or double vision?" Zandra asked.

"No. It was just such a shock. We were struggling against the wind when I was hit. I ended up on the ground, not knowing what happened." Mrs. Simister was small and hunched, dressed in an overly large, dark coat. Her husband wore a rumpled suit and clutched a briefcase to his chest.

"We'll get you better. Take a deep breath and relax. The spell may tickle." Zandra hovered her hand over the woman's injury, and I opened my magic to ensure she had a plentiful supply of power.

"Are you visiting Crimson Cove for pleasure? Or are you here on business?" I nodded at the briefcase the man held.

"We came for the day. We're retired and often go on fun little trips. I'm Doctor Idris Simister. This is my wife." His voice sounded strained as he stared at his injured companion.

"Greetings to you both. I'm sorry we're meeting under these circumstances."

"And I'm sorry if we're inconveniencing you," Doctor Simister said. "But when I saw the lights on, I came straight here. I didn't know what else to do."

"Stay as long as you like." Lila hurried over with a bowl of water and a clean white cloth.

"That's kind of you," Doctor Simister said. "I'm not good with blood, so I had to get help."

"Of course. Your wife will be fine," Zandra said.

"You're not a medical doctor, then?" I asked.

"No! Although, right now, I wish I was. I studied philosophy, for all the good it did me."

"We all need great thinkers," I said.

Doctor Simister barely nodded as he crouched beside his wife, setting down his briefcase.

Once Zandra had finished healing Mrs. Simister, I hopped off her shoulder and walked over to Sage, who stood some distance from the group, looking grumpy. "What's up with you? You barely touched the food. The salmon was delicious."

"One guess. It's covered in fluff and is extremely annoying." She glared at Ember, who was still in Vorana's papoose, his paws and chin resting on the fabric as he took in everything.

"Let's look around on our own. It'll give you something else to think about." I bumped my curmudgeonly friend out of the room, and we crept back up the stairs, Sage using magic to hover her harness behind her so it didn't slow her or scrape the varnished wood.

"I'm beginning to think I'll have to make room for Ember permanently. Vorana clearly loves him," Sage said.

"Almost as much as she loves you. There's room for both of you."

She hissed at me. "I knew you liked him. He fake charms everyone he meets."

"I don't dislike Ember. I do disagree with how he tricked himself into the household, but he's not caused trouble since he arrived. He barely says a word."

"He looks at me funny. And he's irritating. All that pathetic meowing and lifting one paw and begging. He's more like a dog." Sage stopped and stared at the floor. "Look! He's even made a mess in here."

I walked over to see small muddy paw prints drying on the wood. "Are you sure those are his paw prints? Didn't Vorana carry him all the way around?" I checked the bottom of my paws, but they were clean.

"He probably had muddy paws before she picked him up. He's such a messy kitten. And he leaves fur everywhere and never gets told off. But me! I throw up a furball in Vorana's favorite shoe, or leave a dead mouse in her purse, and I get yelled at."

Sage continued to grumble as we looked around the rooms, cursing Ember at every opportunity. I walked across a soft, fluffy rug, enjoying the feel of the wool under my toe beans. A board creaked and dipped under my weight.

I stepped back and forth on it several times. "Help me move this rug."

"Why?" Sage had been exploring underneath the closet.

"There's a loose floorboard."

"So what?" Sage grumbled as she assisted me in dragging the rug to one side. I tugged at the loose board with my paw, digging in my claws so I could lift it.

"Don't damage it," Sage whispered. "If you mess things up, Lila will know we've been poking around."

"Then help me. Wedge your paw under this thing so I can lever it."

"You're always looking for trouble."

"Unfortunately, trouble always seems to find me. And I never duck when presented with a problem."

After a few seconds of pulling, the floorboard moved. I stared at the board, a wave of worry shimmering down my spine. "What are these doing here?"

"Aren't they the markings you've been worried about?" Sage studied the gremlin cult chaos symbols I'd uncovered.

I nodded, fur prickling all over my body. "They're connected to the town's problems. The misbehaving animals, people fighting, and the strange weather."

"Huh! When you told me about them, you never mentioned they could cause so much damage."

"I didn't realize they could. I've been reading up about them, but ever since the town got crazy, I've barely had a moment to think. The more symbols there are, the worse things get." I sniffed the symbols, and a sting of magic frazzled my fur.

"How bad is it gonna get? What's the plan with these things?"

"I'm uncertain what the end goal is. They're omens of misdeed, and their power builds over time. When I first saw them, I wasn't too concerned, but as more have appeared, my concern has grown. And now they're here."

"What does it mean?" Sage asked. "Are they connected to Lila? Did she put them here?"

"She's only just bought the place. Why would she do that?" I sniffed the board tentatively. "Can you remember when Lila moved to Crimson Cove?"

"Not really. I remember Vorana talking about the inn being sold a few months ago. Lila didn't move in straight away, though." Sage sniffed the floorboard, too. "Maybe they were already here. Troublemaking gremlins could have found the inn abandoned and used it as a base while they figured out how to maximize the chaos."

"Why hide the symbols, though? Surely, they'd have daubed them over the walls and ceilings if there was no one around to stop them." I looked around the room. It was an unfinished guest bedroom, neat and freshly painted but lacking any character.

"Do we need to warn our witches about these symbols?" Sage asked. "I don't want Vorana put at any risk."

I nodded. "Something big is coming. Can't you feel it in the air?"

"I feel cold. One second, this place is warm, and the next, it's freezing. There must be a problem with the heating."

"It's more likely to be because Willow has just arrived." I gestured with my chin as the ghost appeared behind Sage.

Sage turned and backed away, her ears lowered.

"Greetings! Don't be afraid of us. We mean no harm," I said to Willow.

The lights in the corridor outside the bedroom flickered for several seconds as she stared at us. "What are you doing in here?"

"Uncovering problems. What do you know about these symbols?"

She blinked slowly several times then inched closer. "The weather is bad."

"It's been bad for weeks," I said. "Is it because of these symbols? They've been appearing all over town."

Willow stared intently at the symbols on the wood. "I don't know what they mean."

"Neither do we. Not exactly, anyway. But it's not a sign good news is coming. Did you see who put them here? Was it gremlins?"

"I... I don't know. I've been here a long time. I lose track of the days and weeks. It all blurs."

"How long have you been trapped here?" Sage asked.

Willow's gaze drifted to the ceiling. "Many years. Hundreds? I worked here. At least, I think I did. So many memories are hazy. No! I did work here. I remember. I must not forget."

"And you really can't move on?" I said. "Do you want to leave?"

"Yes! I've seen too much. It's time for rest."

"Think really hard. Have you any memories of when these symbols were placed here? If it wasn't a gremlin, did you see Lila do it?"

"No. I... I don't think so. But I come and go. And the place has been busy. Too much energy. I don't like it. It worries me and makes me anxious."

"It'll get busier once the inn opens," I said.

Willow shuddered. "I'll be unhappy."

I canted my head to the side. "I may be able to help if you really don't want to stay."

"Help me how?"

"We can work together."

She hesitated. "Doing what?"

"You help us figure out where these symbols came from."

Willow's form flickered like the lights, pulsing in a pleasant, ethereal glow. "Why should I help you? I don't know you. Maybe you put them there."

I gave her a cat smile. "I'd never use such chaotic magic. You must be able to feel the changes. They're connected to these symbols."

A growl of thunder rattled overhead, and the sky lit with a jagged fork of lightning. The wind shook the windows as if trying to find a way in, and the lights wavered again.

"I don't like it. It scares me," Willow said. "Crimson Cove is changing."

"Work with us to stop that from happening," I said. "You help us, and I'll figure out a way to set you free."

"Don't make promises you can't keep," Sage muttered.

Willow's expression brightened. "You can get me out?"

"I'll do my best." Although I'd been limiting my magic use after losing my tail because of a misfiring spell. My powers had been behaving when I'd been working, but I was familiar with using those kinds of spells. Releasing a ghost trapped by an ancient hex would be a stretch, but I'd try.

Willow floated around the room, her fingers sliding along the newly painted white wall.

"Will you help us?" I asked.

"I'd like to leave. I'll help," Willow said.

"Excellent. Let's return to the group before someone notices us missing." I pushed the floorboard back into place, covered it with the rug, and left the room with Sage behind me and Willow floating next to me. "Does Lila ever use unusual magic?"

Willow shook her head. "No, nothing strange. And she prefers potions over spells."

"She's a witch?" Sage said.

Willow nodded. "Kind of. Not a full witch, though."

"I noticed her teeth. Hobgoblin?"

"She never said. Lila uses potions and herbs, but rarely. I don't think she's powerful. What do those symbols do?"

"They conjure chaos. They're from a gremlin cult."

"Oh! I've seen no gremlins here. I've met a few, though. They're noisy and love to scratch and chew on things. They make a mess. I'd know if a gremlin had visited."

"Were you a witch when alive?" I asked.

"A weak one. I wasn't good at anything, so I worked here in the kitchens, but I always burned the toast." Willow made a noise of surprise. "My memories are clearer now we're talking."

"It helps to share with others." I'd also ensured she could freely access my energy to give her a boost.

Willow slid me some side-eye. "I suppose it does. My lack of talent embarrassed my parents. I watched them at my funeral as they whispered to each other that if I'd been a better witch, I'd never have become trapped." She waved a hand in the air, and the scent of burned toast drifted around us.

"I believe in you," I said. "We'll figure out what's going on with the symbols and then you'll be free to do what you like."

Willow's smile was cautiously optimistic.

We returned to the group to find Mrs. Simister looking brighter now her head wound had been healed. She had a mug of tea beside her and a plate piled with food from the buffet, which she greedily devoured, scattering crumbs down the front of her coat.

Her husband was also taking his fill, stuffing food into his mouth in big noisy bites.

Gaian and Sorcha stood apart from the rest of the group, talking quietly to each other. Zandra was with Vorana and Ember on the other side of the room, standing close to Doctor and Mrs. Simister. Lila was chatting to Finn and Cythera, showing them some polished wood carvings close to the large open fireplace.

I looked around the assembled group, and my gaze settled on Gaian and Sorcha. I'd always had my doubts about him. He had power, which I'd seen displayed when he'd gone up against Remus at the Blood Moon Festival. He also had the power to charm and manipulate, as witnessed through the unfortunate changes in Sorcha's business affairs and personal life. When they got together, he'd seemed good for her, but now she was tense and anxious. And every time I thought about the café, I felt queasy. All that lost salmon.

I looked at Lila next. This was her inn, so I had to consider her involvement in those symbols. And she'd arrived around the same time the symbols first showed up.

My gaze flicked to Doctor and Mrs. Simister. They were strangers, shoved into the inn by accident rather than design.

Mrs. Simister finished her plate of food and filled it again. Maybe the shock of being whacked in the head with a rock made her hungry.

"What are you thinking?" Sage had remained by my side while Willow drifted off and floated around the group.

"We focus on Gaian. The trouble started after he arrived. And why is he here tonight? To check his symbols are having the desired effect?"

"Lila must have invited him. I think she invited everyone who has a business."

"Gaian's not a sociable guy. What does he gain from coming here?"

Sage grunted. "He's not a gremlin, though. He's a warlock."

"Maybe a warlock who's using different magic to extend his influence. Gaian needed a power base to expand from, and when he met Sorcha, he realized she lived in the perfect location. Crimson Cove is full of powerful magical beings." I glared at him as he kissed Sorcha's head. "Why not exploit another magic user's tricks? When you know how to use the chaos symbols, they'll work for you if you have enough magic."

"If you're looking for suspects, you need to include Ember," Sage said. "That little sneak has been a problem ever since I met him."

"But you sought him out. You thought Vorana needed a new familiar and went to the academy to find one. Gaian insinuated himself into Sorcha's life deliberately."

"What's to say Ember didn't do that with me? He manipulated his application because he wanted to get a paw in the door of Crimson Cove. He's sly enough to do it."

I glanced at my grouchy friend. "You're biased when it comes to that kitten."

"So are you with Gaian. You hate that the café is plant-based, and you can't get salmon on tap whenever you like."

I grudgingly admitted Sage was right. I had an issue with Gaian, but it was more than his manipulation of the menu at my once favorite café. He'd changed Sorcha beyond recognition, isolated her from her friends, and he was smug and superior, acting as if his values were more important than anyone else's.

"Let's admit, we both have bias in this situation," I said.

"They're both suspects, though? We can't trust Ember."

"They have to be." I wouldn't air my doubts about Ember as a suspect, and he had arrived around the time the symbols became a problem, so there was an outside chance he was involved.

"Please, help yourselves to more food." Lila turned from her conversation with Finn and Cythera to address the group. "I've catered for lots more people than this, so it'll only go to waste."

"You don't have to ask me twice." Mrs. Simister grabbed another plate of food. She also grabbed a second empty plate and filled it with desserts before returning to her seat.

Everyone else headed to the buffet, and I was pleased Zandra got more salmon for me.

"How will we handle this?" Sage asked. "Should I confront Ember? Grab him by his scruff and shake the truth out of him about those symbols."

"We must be discreet. Ask a few questions during casual conversations. It's not as if we can say we were snooping and discovered the symbols hidden under the floor." I edged closer to Zandra, eager to eat the salmon.

"What if we don't learn anything? It's not as if the culprit will reveal they snuck up there and left them."

"We have Willow on our side. She can listen to conversations and hear if anything strange is talked about. We'll get her to focus on Gaian."

"And Ember. Don't forget him."

"I'll hardly do that with you reminding me how awful he is. Let's grab food then get to work."

The wind slammed into the building so hard it shook the overhead lights on their gold chains. The windows rattled, and there was an enormous growl of thunder followed by more lightning.

Lila hurried to the window and peered out. "We may need to cut this evening short. I don't want any of you getting hurt when you go home."

"If it's not too much trouble, we'd like to stay the night," Doctor Simister said.

Lila turned from the window and raised her eyebrows. "I'm not ready for guests. I haven't even taken my first booking."

"We'll be no trouble. I'd just like my wife to have a proper rest." Doctor Simister placed a hand on his wife's shoulder. "You won't even know we're here."

Lila pursed her lips then nodded. "I'm sure we can sort something out. It won't be a luxurious experience, though. And I'm not sure you'll get a good night's sleep with the wind attacking the inn. It seems determined to get inside."

"I'm a sound sleeper," Mrs. Simister said. "Once my head hits the pillow, nothing wakes me. Not even my husband's snoring."

Lila's smile was tight as she gestured to the buffet again. "Eat your fill. Then I'll prepare a room for you."

Doctor and Mrs. Simister nodded eagerly then dashed back to the buffet.

I was heading over to Zandra when there was another vicious howl of wind. The lights flickered, and there was a snarl of thunder. I'd taken two more paw steps when the lights flickered again then blinked out, leaving the room in ominous darkness. There were several squeaks and a couple of nervous laughs.

"Don't panic! I've got a torch somewhere. Could someone cast a light ball? Ouch!" Lila cursed. "I can't see a thing."

Something creaked. No, cracked. A loud, ominous crack that echoed through the blackness, making my fur fluff. An object swooped past my face and smashed onto the floor so hard the boards bounced under my paws.

The lights flickered back on to reveal an old, heavy wooden ceiling beam had come loose. And Doctor Simister was squashed underneath it.

Chapter 4

Dead before dawn

A few heartbeats passed as everyone processed the horrifying scene. I checked where Zandra was, relieved to find her on the other side of the beam, her eyes wide with shock.

"Idris? Are you hurt?" Mrs. Simister's plate of food hit the floor. She dropped to her knees and scrambled toward him. "Help me! We need to move this beam. He can't get out."

Everyone sprang into action. Cythera and Finn positioned themselves at either end of the beam and lifted on a count of three. Gaian, Zandra, Vorana, and Sorcha also helped as they moved the beam to the side and dropped it on the floor.

Sage nudged me. "He's not coming back from that. Not even magic can bring back someone that squished. He looks like roadkill."

I had to agree as a pungent metallic tang filled the air. The beam had covered Doctor Simister, not an inch of him spared as it dropped from the ceiling. What I hadn't been able to see until the beam was lifted were the small white glowing gremlin chaos symbols printed on his forehead. My heart stuttered.

"Help him!" Mrs. Simister cried repeatedly. "Idris! Idris! You'll be fine. Oh, dear. No! Help!"

"I think it's too late." Vorana settled a hand on the crying woman's shoulder. "There's nothing anyone can do."

"No! He just needs medical help. He'll be fine. Do you have a hospital?"

Vorana looked around the group, her expression tight. "We do. But—"

"We take him there. They'll fix him." Mrs. Simister's hand hovered over her dead husband's cheek. "We'll get you back on your feet in no time. You promised me a fine dining experience before we leave. You never break your promises."

"Um... it may not be that easy to help him." Finn approached her cautiously, his wings lowered in a show of remorse.

"It will! If no one will help me, I'll take him myself. Tell me where to go." Mrs. Simister wobbled to her feet, a defiant look in her damp eyes.

"We'll help. Of course." Cythera strode over. "Flight won't be possible because of the wind, but we'll have someone translocate you and your husband to our medical facility. They'll do what they can for him."

"Yes! Good. Now! We must go now." Mrs. Simister wiped her eyes with the back of her hand and gestured at the door.

Finn looked at Zandra. "Can you help?"

I hurried to my witch and leaped onto her shoulder. "Let's get them out of here. Then figure out what happened. And I want a closer look at those symbols."

She nodded, set down her plate of food, absently grabbing a piece of smoked salmon and feeding it to me. "Sure. Let's go."

I gobbled the salmon as Zandra edged around the beam, the end jagged with splinters and deep grooves gouging the ancient wood, and rested her hands on Mrs. Simister and her late husband.

"We'll meet you at the hospital," Finn said. "We may have to travel on foot, so we'll be a few minutes."

Zandra nodded. "We'll wait with Mrs. Simister until you arrive."

I felt her magic unfurl and the translocation spell take hold. We didn't move. I leaned closer to the body. The symbols were still there. Who had done that to Doctor Simister?

Zandra drew in a deep breath and tried again. Nothing.

"Why aren't we going anywhere?" Mrs. Simister said. "This is an emergency!"

"The spell won't take hold," Zandra said.

"It's working. I can feel it." I added a boost of power to the mix. "Try again."

Zandra gritted her teeth and pushed more of her own magic into the spell. She let out a breath. "Nope. I'm getting nothing."

"It feels as if something is blocking our magic." My toe beans were sweating from forcing the spell to work. "I felt a push back when you cast the translocation spell."

"Are you sure you're doing it right?" Gaian said.

I didn't waste a glare on him for asking such a stupid question.

"Someone else try," Zandra said. "We've been using a lot of magic at work. I know I need rest before I'm fully charged."

"You're more powerful than me, even when you're having an off day," Vorana said. "I'm happy to give it a go, but if you can't do it, I won't be able to."

"Don't underestimate yourself," Ember said. "You can do much more than you realize. You've been held back for too long."

"That's sweet. But I know my limits." Vorana glanced at Sorcha, but she shrugged and looked away, not willing to help.

"Let me do it." Gaian pushed up his sleeves and strode over.

"I'm telling you, something is blocking the magic." Zandra reluctantly shuffled out of his way, not pleased at having to yield to this smug warlock. "Maybe it's those symbols."

Gaian cracked his knuckles. "You're just tired. You know, you look pale. Not been eating enough steak? Isn't that where you carnivores get your iron from?"

"My witch looks like perfection." I growled at Gaian. "You should show deference to a magic user from such an ancient and well-respected family. If you don't, another Crypt witch may smite you."

Gaian smirked as he placed a hand on Doctor Simister's shoulder. "Let me do the heavy lifting. This is man's work."

"What a jerk," Zandra muttered under her breath.

As much as I wanted Doctor Simister's body removed, I secretly hoped Gaian's spell would fail and knock him on his butt, leaving behind a giant bruise that would make it impossible for him to sit down for a week.

He cracked his neck, then his fingers again, and returned his hand to the corpse. No one spoke as we waited for Gaian to disappear with the body and Mrs. Simister.

Nothing happened.

"Is there a problem?" I said in my most innocent tone.

"It must be the weather interfering with my magic. That storm is something else." Gaian had his eyes closed, and a trickle of sweat ran down the side of his face.

I leaned in close to Zandra. "He can't do it."

"Which is satisfying to watch, but why can't any of us translocate out of here?" Zandra whispered. "It's not a difficult spell."

I glanced into the gloomy night as a crackle of lightning split the sky and outlined the rain-laden clouds that sat heavy above our heads. "There's nothing natural about this weather. Someone has created this storm. Maybe they've cast more chaotic spells that are messing with us."

"Something was repelling the magic, squeezing it and stopping it from working," Zandra muttered.

"What have you got around this place?" Gaian opened his eyes and stared at Lila. "Some kind of containment spell?"

She shook her head. "Why would I do that? I sent invitations to over fifty businesses, so I expected people to come and go all evening."

"There's something stopping the magic from working." Gaian glanced at me and Zandra, his expression less than happy. "If we want to move the body, we'll have to do it the old-fashioned way."

"Please, I need my husband taken care of," Mrs. Simister said. "He must be revived."

"What do you know about those symbols on his face?" I asked.

She jumped. "I... oh! I didn't notice. I mean, I did, but... please. Help me."

Finn gently touched her shoulder. "I'm sorry, but given the injuries your husband sustained when that beam fell on him, nothing will bring him back. Even if the doctor performed miraculous healing magic, Doctor Simister wouldn't have been the same. You wouldn't want him brought back differently or damaged, would you?"

Mrs. Simister's shoulders sagged, and tears dripped off her chin. "I need to be sure there's nothing that'll help him."

"We'll find something suitable to cover him and take him ourselves," Cythera said. "He'll be treated with the greatest of respect."

"I've got blankets," Lila said. "We could wrap them around him."

"Yes! I'd like him covered and kept warm." Mrs. Simister sniffed.

Lila hurried off to get the blankets.

I inspected the jagged end of the beam closest to Doctor Simister's head. Deep score marks covered the wood. Gaian was also looking at them.

"You've got a problem in this place," he said to Lila as she returned with an armful of dark green woolen blankets. "This wood looks damaged. Maybe even rotten."

"What do you mean?" Lila said.

Gaian tilted his head as he continued his inspection of the beam. "Maybe not rotten. It could have been faulty renovation work that did this."

Lila dropped the blankets. "I paid a fortune to have this place restored. Nothing is faulty or rotten."

As much as it pained me to agree with Gaian, the marks in the wood looked like someone had made them deliberately. And with the appearance of those gremlin symbols on Doctor Simister's face, this death didn't seem like an accident.

Lila strode over to inspect the beam, and her face paled. "I don't know how they got there. The wood looks... torn."

"You could have termites," Gaian said.

"They'd have to be giant termites with werewolf claws to do that much damage," I muttered.

Lila stepped back, shaking her head. "The beams are safe. I had them checked and even a few reinforced." Her gaze went to the ceiling. "I have no idea how this one came loose."

"Let's not worry about that now," Cythera said. While Lila and Gaian had examined the fallen beam, Mrs. Simister, Cythera, and Finn had wrapped Doctor Simister in the blankets.

Finn lifted him into his arms, and Cythera strode to the main door. She tried the handle.

"We need the key," she said.

"It's unlocked," Lila said.

Cythera tried again. "It isn't."

"I'm sure I left it unlocked. Let me try. Sometimes, the wood warps and sticks when it's been raining." She hurried over and tried the handle, twisting it several times. She pulled a key from her pocket and fitted it into the lock. "I knew it wasn't locked. Why won't it open?"

A shiver of unease swirled around my stomach. "Is there another way out?"

"There's the back door." Lila hurried past us, heading along the corridor and into the kitchen. She flicked on an overhead light to reveal a spacious room with high ceilings and dark, richly painted amber walls. An ornate chandelier hung from the ceiling, casting warm light over the space. The countertops were dark stone.

Lila jogged to a door and attempted to open it. It wouldn't budge. She tugged on it several times. "I know I didn't lock this door because I wanted to show off the canopied seating area for guests."

"Let me try." Gaian walked over, flexing his muscles. He was equally unsuccessful in getting the door open.

"I have a bad feeling about this," I murmured to Zandra from my position on her shoulder.

"We're stuck here," Mrs. Simister wailed. "Why are you trapping us in here?" She jabbed a finger at Lila.

"I'm not! I want to get out as much as you." Lila stared at the keys in her hand, an expression of concern causing her forehead to wrinkle.

"Perhaps the inn doesn't want us to leave," I said. "It's locked us inside."

"Don't be so dramatic," Cythera said. "We'll try all available exits. Doors and windows. Are there more doors?"

"Just the front and back. But we can try the windows," Lila said.

"We'll take the upstairs with Vorana," Cythera said. "The rest of you look around down here and find a way out." She strode off. Finn and Vorana followed her. Ember was in his papoose, and Sage was hot on Vorana's heels.

Gaian and Sorcha headed back to the front of the building while I remained with Mrs. Simister and Zandra. We started in the kitchen, testing the windows. They were stuck just as tight. We found three storerooms and a messy office. The windows also refused to budge.

Although Mrs. Simister stayed with us, she didn't attempt to open any windows. She was too busy snuffling back tears and wiping her eyes. "This was supposed to be a fun day out. It shouldn't have ended like this."

"I'm sorry it has." I jumped off Zandra's shoulder and gently nudged Mrs. Simister's calf with my head. "But we'll soon find a way out and get your husband to the hospital."

"How? Nothing opens. Lila has trapped us in here. Why would she do that?"

"We don't know she's behind this," Zandra said. "As you've probably noticed, things are strange in Crimson Cove."

"I said to Idris we should leave when the weather got worse, but he said we'd wait for it to blow over then go on our walk as we'd planned. I should have been firmer. Stood up to him, but he always did what he wanted. Now look what's happened. He's dead!" She wiped the sleeve of her coat across her face several times.

"We should try magic to make an exit," I said to Zandra. "Lila won't mind if we inflict a little damage if it gets us free."

We returned to the back door, and Zandra fired up an unlock spell. She rested her hand on the doorknob and pulsed out the magic.

"Anything happening?" I asked.

Zandra froze, yelped, and flew back. She lay in a groaning heap, her hands clutching her chest.

I dashed to my witch and leapt on her arm. "What happened?"

"It felt as if something bit me." She slowly lifted her hand and inspected it. There were deep bleeding holes across her palm as if a mean spirited, sharp-toothed predator had attacked her.

"That looks like an animal bite." Mrs. Simister stared down at Zandra. "That happened because you used a spell to get us out?"

I licked Zandra's hand until the wound vanished. "Stay here. I'll try. No stinking magic hurts my witch and gets away with it."

"Be careful," Zandra said. "The spell that whacked me felt awful. My stomach is still churning."

Fury roiled through me as I stomped to the door and glared at the offending handle. I dug deep into my well of ancient power. "Don't let me down. I need you firing out of every magical cylinder. We aren't staying trapped in this haunted inn for a second longer than we have to." I drew in a deep breath, closed my eyes, and centered my power on breaking through the door. Rather than using an unlock spell, I sent out something more vicious. A spell that would blast an enormous hole through the wood.

The magic built inside me, warming me from my toe beans to the tips of my ears. I threw it out, and it slammed into the door then rebounded and smashed into me.

I howled as I was flung through the air, saved by my wonderful witch as she caught me in a firm grip and drew me against her chest. I hissed and howled, unable to control myself as my limbs shook while the spell ricocheted through me, pinging against bone and sinew like hot little daggers.

"Is she alive?" Mrs. Simister said.

"Barely," I grumbled.

Zandra held me tight, gently stroking me until my heartbeat slowed. "Whatever magic has trapped us, it isn't playing nice."

I rested in my witch's arms, embarrassed and angry in equal measure that I'd failed to get us free.

There was a strangled yelp, and something heavy hit the floor above our heads.

"Sounds like other people are trying the same thing," I said. "Mrs. Simister, perhaps you should warn them not to use magic."

"Oh! Of course. We don't want anyone else getting hurt." She hurried out of the kitchen.

"If we can't get out, maybe someone can get in," I said. "We need to call for help."

"I was thinking the same thing." Zandra already had her mobile snow globe in one hand. "I'll call Tia. She's not far from here." She made the connection, but it dropped instantly. She tried several more times but got the same response. Then she tried Voss Black at the pizza parlor, then the Angel Force main number. None of the connections held.

My gaze went to the inky night sky, and I resisted the desire to recoil. Everything felt wrong about this situation, and I didn't want to stay here a moment longer than we had to.

"Could the weather be messing with our communication network?" Zandra glared at her mobile snow globe.

"I'm not sure. Let's find Vorana and Sage. We need to discuss this problem with people we trust."

"What about Cythera and Finn?"

"We'll get to them. I don't want Cythera steamrollering our ideas until we have a fully formed action plan."

We left the kitchen and met the rest of the group as they returned from their unsuccessful endeavors to get out. Finn had a burned wing, Gaian was holding his ribs, and Sage's fur was fluffed and singed.

"You tried to use magic, too?" I asked.

"Yes, and the inn wasn't happy about it," Vorana said. "I got a pile of books thrown at my head. Almost knocked me out."

"Let's go back to the dining room," Gaian said. "I've got an idea for how to fix this mess."

"If it involves getting people from the outside to help, you're out of luck," I said. "Communications are down."

He stopped in the doorway. "Who have you tried to reach?"

"Friends and Angel Force," Zandra said.

"I have better contacts. I'll reach them. Everyone, follow me." Gaian turned and walked into the dining room with Sorcha beside him. After a moment of hesitation, the others followed.

Zandra caught hold of Vorana's arm. "Before we join them, we need to talk."

"Do you know what's going on?" she whispered.

"Let's find somewhere quiet, where we can't be overheard," I said. "I'm not sure who I trust in this group."

For once, Ember wasn't attached to Vorana, so we could talk just the four of us. Sage, of course, was there, never far from her beloved witch's side.

"Let's start in a guest bedroom," I said. "There's something you need to see."

We hurried up the stairs, aware we had little time before Gaian realized we weren't part of his loyal gang. I directed Zandra to the room and got her to pull up the floorboard to reveal the symbols.

"Those are the gremlin symbols you've been asking about," Vorana said. "You were researching them in the bookstore a few weeks ago."

"What are they doing here?" Zandra asked.

"They're here to show we're in deep trouble. I think these symbols, Doctor Simister's death, and the chaos outside are connected. We have a murder on our paws. And since the killer has trapped us here, they may just be getting started."

Chapter 5
The mystery deepens

According to the clock, dawn was breaking, although it was so gloomy outside, you wouldn't know it. After fruitless attempts to contact anyone outside the inn by all members of the group, we'd bedded down and gotten some rest.

There'd been limited options for sleeping, since most of the rooms were unfurnished, so Sorcha, Gaian, Vorana, Sage, and Ember shared a small family room. Lila had slept in her office, and I was in with Zandra, Mrs. Simister, Finn, and Cythera. It had made for a less than pleasant sleeping experience, since Cythera snored. Not that I'd been able to sleep much as I'd mulled over the events of the previous evening.

Finn yawned and rolled out of the chair he'd chosen to sleep in. He cracked just about every ligament and fluttered his wings, stretching each one.

He gave me a sleepy grin when he saw me watching. "I've had better nights' sleep." He walked to the sash window and attempted to open it. "Still stuck."

Mrs. Simister, who'd been given the only bed, sat up with a sigh. "I'll use the bathroom first. If you'll excuse me." She padded barefoot into the attached bathroom and closed the door.

I prodded Zandra with a paw until she opened her eyes. "While Mrs. Simister is out of the room, I thought we should talk."

Cythera sat up from the couch. "I suppose you've worked out some genius way to get out of here."

"No, I'm as stumped as everyone else as to why we're trapped. But I didn't have the chance to speak to either of you last night about the symbols I found." Although Cythera underrated my genius, I trusted both angels, and I needed them onside so we could figure out what was going on.

"Is the situation we've found ourselves in going to turn into another of your great conspiracy theories?" Cythera stretched her wings and adjusted a few feathers that had become ruffled while she slept.

"It's a conspiracy fact! We're in the middle of a troubling situation." I briefly washed my face with a paw, making sure not to miss my ears. "Yesterday, I discovered gremlin chaos symbols hidden under a floorboard in a guest bedroom. And then, they appeared on Doctor Simister after he got crushed! That's no coincidence."

"Why were you poking around under the inn's floorboards?" Cythera said.

"You're missing the point. They're the same symbols that have been showing up all over town.

Those symbols are linked to the troubles we're having. Not just getting locked in here, but all the lawbreaking and chaotic animals." I glared at Cythera until she stopped preening her wings. "I've tried to talk to you about the symbols several times, but you've given me the brushoff. Now, we find ourselves here."

"Because they're not important," Cythera said. "I looked into them. They come from a defunct gremlin cult that died out hundreds of years ago. No one uses them anymore. They have no power."

I was surprised she'd bother to do any investigation. "Someone is using them. Someone has started the cult again, and they have their sights set on Crimson Cove. And somehow, whoever is making those symbols is linked to this inn. Why else would they hide symbols here?"

"Do you think Lila is involved?" Finn said.

"It could be Gaian," Zandra said. "Last night, we were discussing with Vorana and Sage who could be involved. Those symbols showed up around the time the gang did."

"I've spoken to Gaian and his gang about the graffiti. They assured me they had nothing to do with it," Cythera said. "And, before you make assumptions that I haven't been doing my job, I've had my angels look into the individual gang members' backgrounds. Many of them have troubled pasts, but none of their crimes are serious. And none of them have connections to gremlin cults. They're a mixture of warlocks and witches. Most of them aren't powerful."

"Gaian is powerful," I said. "We've seen his showy displays of supernatural strength. What's to say he hasn't co-opted those chaos-making symbols?"

"For what purpose?" Cythera said. "As frustrating as I find some of Gaian's behavior, he seeks to do good in the world."

"Since he's moved here, things haven't changed for the better," I said.

"Only because you don't like tofu burgers," Cythera said. "I've heard you griping about the lack of fish in the café. It's childish. You shouldn't use your personal issues with Gaian to make him a suspect in this situation."

"I'm not! But I'm also not a big believer in coincidences. His gang shows up, and the symbols appear. And now, they're on a dead body."

"He's not my favorite person," Finn said, "but he respects the law. I've had to speak to him a few times when his actions have entered shady territory, and he always backs down and changes his plans. It seems out of character that he'd do something as dramatic as reviving an old gremlin cult."

I huffed a snort of disgust. I couldn't believe everyone was on Gaian's side. Why couldn't they see what he was?

"What about Lila?" Finn said. "I'm not sure when she bought this place, but she's been around for a few months. Does that tie in to when the symbols showed up and the trouble began?"

"That's assuming there's a connection," Cythera said.

I didn't want to be distracted from my focus on Gaian, but Finn made a valid point. Cythera, not so much. "It's possible Lila showing up has something to do with this."

"Especially since we found hidden symbols right here," Zandra said.

"If we could make contact with someone at Angel Force, we could run a background check on Lila and find out more about her," Cythera said. "But while we're stuck here, there's little we can do."

"There's plenty we can do," I said. "We're trapped in here with a murderer. And they're not getting out either."

"When did we start talking murder?" Cythera said.

"You saw the beam that fell on Doctor Simister. The gouge marks on the end didn't get there by accident. Someone damaged that beam."

"Why would anyone want to kill him?" Finn asked. "He was just visiting town with his wife for the day. No one knew them."

"Maybe so. But an unexpected murder causes chaos," I said. "That's what those symbols are all about. Gaian is using them to maximize fear, uncertainty, and trouble before he makes his next devious move."

"If it even is Gaian," Cythera said. "You can't keep jumping to these over-the-top assumptions. We don't know what the symbols mean. We don't know who's putting them around town, and we don't even know if Doctor Simister was murdered."

"We have the evidence downstairs. Why not investigate? There's nothing else to do while we're trapped."

Cythera was looking at her mobile snow globe. "Once this storm dies down, we should be able to get a connection. We can get someone to break down the door from the outside."

"So long as the magic trapping us doesn't kill them while they do it," I said. "We need to find out who's behind this chaos and get them to remove the barrier. Let's start with Mrs. Simister. Find out more about her background. She may have helpful information about her husband. Maybe give us a connection that ties him to Crimson Cove and a reason someone targeted him."

"By dropping an enormous wooden beam on him?" Finn shook his head. "Why use such a cumbersome weapon?"

"To find that out, we need to question the suspects," I said.

Cythera tutted. "Suspects? There are no suspects."

The lights flickered, and the temperature dropped just as Willow floated through the wall. She stared at everyone. "Am I interrupting? I can leave if you don't want me here."

"Your timing is perfect," I said. "We were discussing last night's events. Perhaps you overheard something to help us figure out what happened to Doctor Simister."

Willow inched back toward the wall. "No! Nothing. I came to see if anyone was awake. The others are up."

"You're sure? I didn't see much of you last night. You weren't around when we were attempting to get out."

"I find crowds troubling. I prefer my own company." Willow's hands were clasped together.

"You'll help us figure this out, though, won't you?" Willow had been anxious the first time we met, but her anxiety had gone up several notches overnight.

Her gaze flashed to the window. "I hate this weather. It unsettles me. Makes me feel out of control."

"Does it make you act erratically?" Cythera said. "Make you do things you shouldn't?"

Willow's eyes widened. "I... I... No! I have to go." She turned and shot through the wall.

"Nicely interrogated," I said to Cythera.

"You said we needed to gather information from the suspects. You're telling me Willow isn't a suspect because she's a ghost?"

I held in an exasperated sigh. "Willow agreed to help us look into what's going on. We've already made a deal. I'll free her from her hex, and in return, she'll keep track of everyone's movements and see if anyone says or does anything strange. You've just ruined that deal by terrifying her. She may not show up anymore in case a grumpy angel grouses at her."

"It serves you right for making deals behind my back. How was I supposed to know?"

"That's our fault." Zandra leapt to my defense. "We just want to figure out what's going on quickly so we can get out of here. Juno was being proactive."

"It's one of my many qualities," I said.

"And we love that about you," Finn said. "But keep us informed about your schemes so we don't tread on your paws and scare any more informants."

"Agreed and understood. Now, who's questioning Mrs. Simister when she comes out of the bathroom? Shall I? She needs to be handled sensitively."

"No interrogation," Cythera said. "If you must speak to her, keep it casual. We don't want to alarm anyone by talking about murder when we don't know what happened to Doctor Simister."

"I'm happy to talk to her. She's a sweet old lady," I said. "But what will you do? May I suggest—"

"We'll find Lila. Ask about her background." Cythera wrinkled her nose as if she'd just smelled a rotten fish. "This had better not be a waste of my time."

"And maybe find breakfast?" Finn said. "I'd kill for a coffee."

Cythera smoothed down her hair, gestured for Finn to follow her, and left the room. Finn grinned at us then hurried out.

A moment later, the bathroom door opened and Mrs. Simister came out, her face pink from where she'd washed it. "All yours. The water's nice and hot."

"Thanks. How are you feeling?" I asked.

"Like I'm coming out of some terrible dream." Mrs. Simister settled on the edge of the bed. "We'd been together over fifty years. Although that man irritated me beyond belief sometimes, I don't know what I'll do without him. We did nearly everything together after he retired." She dabbed at her eyes with a hand towel she'd brought from the bathroom.

"We are sorry for your loss." Zandra perched on the bed next to Mrs. Simister.

"I just want to take him home. I know there's nothing I can do now, but I need to be with him so I can mourn in private. I can't do that while we're trapped here."

"Cythera and Finn have gone to see how things are downstairs," I said. "Perhaps they'll have good news and Lila has figured out a way to get the doors open. They were talking about breakfast, too, if you're hungry."

"I can't eat. I can barely think straight. I just want out of here." Mrs. Simister hopped off the bed, hurried to the window, and thrust out her hands, magic rising from her palms.

Zandra dashed after her. "Don't you remember what happened to me and Juno?"

"I must try!" Mrs. Simister zapped out a spell. It whacked against the window, shimmered in an arc, and slammed into her hands. She staggered back, doubling over and groaning, her hands tucked under her armpits as her body shook.

"Let me see. Did you get bitten too?" Zandra gently tugged on Mrs. Simister's arm.

She resisted for a second but then dropped a hand. It was covered in a shimmering green haze, the skin pulsing and undulating in an unpleasantly distorted wave.

"That's different," I murmured. "Zandra got bitten, I got stung, and you changed color."

"It's already wearing off. I'll be fine." Mrs. Simister pulled her sleeve over her hand. "I'm a stupid old woman for even trying. I'm not powerful. Neither was Idris. We used magic less and less as we got older because it took so much out of us." Mrs. Simister sighed. "If a young witch like you can't break through, I have no hope. But I don't want to give up on Idris. He deserves better."

"I know it's not nice to talk about last night, but I can't stop thinking about those marks on your husband's face," I said. "Have you ever seen them before?"

"It's a mystery to me as well. I was thinking about them while I was trying to sleep. I don't know where they came from. Were they on the wooden beam that struck him?" Her eyes watered. "None of this makes any sense. I just want to return to bed and forget we ever came here."

"Let's go downstairs and join the others," I said. "Maybe you'll feel better when you've had a cup of coffee and something to eat."

"I won't feel better until I've found out what happened to my husband." Mrs. Simister trudged to the door. "But some toast would be nice."

Zandra tugged on her boots and straightened her rumpled sweater before she guided Mrs. Simister out of the bedroom and toward the stairs. "Do you know anyone in Crimson Cove? When we get out of here, you might like to spend time with a friend. You don't want to be alone at a time like this."

"No, as I said, we were here for a fun day trip. We know no one here."

"What line of business was your husband in? Did he ever do business in Crimson Cove?" I asked as we walked down the stairs.

"Nothing exciting. He was a salesman. He was such a gentle man. Kind to everyone, even those who didn't deserve it. I can't think of anyone who disliked him." Mrs. Simister exhaled heavily.

We stopped by the entrance to the dining room.

"He's still in there?" Mrs. Simister's bottom lip wobbled.

"He is," I said. "Do you want to see him?"

She lowered her head. "It's such a tragedy. Although... I overheard Gaian talking about cheap labor. The renovation work not being done properly. Is that true?"

"Ignore him. That's Gaian blowing hot air," I said.

"He said something about marks on the beam that hit my husband. What if it was poor quality building work? Maybe Lila is responsible for what happened." Mrs. Simister sucked in a wobbly breath and drew back her shoulders. "If I find out—"

"What?" Lila stalked out of the kitchen, rage infusing her cheeks bright red. "What will you do if you believe I killed your husband?"

Chapter 6

Heated encounter

Lila stomped along the hallway, her eyes blazing as she confronted Mrs. Simister. "Well? If you have a problem with me, let's hear it."

Mrs. Simister's cheeks grew pink, but she didn't drop eye contact with Lila. "I'm only saying what other people have been talking about. That beam was damaged. Maybe not even repaired while you were renovating this place. Did you hire cheap labor to do the work?"

"No! I want this inn to be incredible. I wouldn't cut a few corners to save money and put my guests at risk."

"Then explain how a ceiling beam squashed my husband."

"I can't! I'm as stunned as everyone else. And I already told Gaian that an expert checked the woodwork."

"What expert? Tell me who they are. I insist on speaking to them to find out if you're telling the truth."

Lila's hands balled into fists. "Why would I lie?"

"To save your business! When word gets out that my husband was killed here because of your incompetence, no one will book a room. You'll be finished."

"Ladies, everyone is tense because of this situation," I said, "but we don't know all the facts. This may have been a tragic accident." Although I was convinced it wasn't, I didn't want to distress Mrs. Simister any more than she already was.

"Whatever happened, I still don't have a husband." Mrs. Simister's voice wobbled along with her knees.

Lila's anger faded. "I'm sorry this happened, but it wasn't because of anything I did. This place is my pride and joy. I've thrown all the money I had into it and then some."

"It's been an expensive project?" I asked.

"What if it has?" Lila glared at me. "It was worth it. I showed my family I was a successful businesswoman and people could take me seriously. That's all I've ever wanted. I wouldn't jeopardize this opportunity by scrimping on the work. That would only land me in trouble."

"It has landed you in trouble," Mrs. Simister said. "You've had a death in this place before it's even opened. That won't get you a gold star recommendation. I want justice for my husband."

"I can't give that to you, since I wasn't involved with his death." Lila's nostrils flared. "He was in the wrong place at the wrong time. It could have been any of us that got hit with the beam."

"You're saying this was his fault?"

"No! It was no one's fault. That's my point. No one is to blame. An accident happened. A sad, horrible accident, but that's all it was."

"You don't understand how I'm feeling." Mrs. Simister sniffed back tears.

Lila pressed her fingers against her forehead. "No, not exactly, but I can see you're upset and angry, and you have every right to be. But it's unfair to pin the blame on me."

"Someone must be held responsible."

"As soon as we get out of here, Angel Force will look into things and make sure everything was done properly," Zandra said.

"If you're referring to my business, everything was done properly." Lila flung an icy glare at her. "I'm not getting in trouble for something I haven't done. I've got enough problems to deal with."

"You're treating my husband's death as an inconvenience to your bottom line." Mrs. Simister scowled at her. "You cold, unfeeling creature. I will have justice for Idris's death." She raised her hand and flung a waft of green magic at Lila.

Lila squeaked and dodged out of the way. "You crazy old woman! If I could, I'd throw you out."

"Try it! I'd love to see the inn bite you. It's no less than you deserve."

I glanced up at Zandra, and we exchanged a nod. I headed over to Lila, while Zandra cut off Mrs. Simister before she could toss out more spells.

"Lila, is that the delicious scent of frying bacon wafting in the air?" I asked.

She glowered at Mrs. Simister for a few seconds before glancing down at me. "Sure. That was what

I was coming to tell you. I made breakfast. There's no reason we should go hungry while we wait for this magic barrier to come down. I didn't expect to overhear this old baggage accusing me of killing her husband."

"How dare you! I'm a grieving widow. I'm allowed to wonder what happened to poor Idris."

Zandra caught hold of Mrs. Simister's elbow. "Let's take a walk. We can look around the guest sitting room, and we'll have a good view of the street from there, so we can see if the weather has improved, or signal to any people walking by that we need help."

The wind howled and rattled the windows as if to prove that it was as dreadful as it had been the previous night.

Mrs. Simister resisted for a few seconds then sighed and allowed Zandra to lead her away but kept muttering under her breath and glaring at Lila over her shoulder as they disappeared into the sitting room.

Lila huffed out several breaths. "The nerve of that woman. I've put my all into this place. All the money I had, all the free time, all the hassle that goes into starting a business." She took off along the corridor and headed toward the kitchen.

I followed her. "It sounds stressful."

Lila grabbed a sizzling pan on the hob and flipped pieces of crispy bacon. "And then some. This is the last thing I need. Two strangers blundering in and spoiling things. Last night was supposed to be about making connections with local business owners so we could share the word about each other, and I could drum up trade. Then those two walk in and disaster strikes." She was so vigorously flipping the bacon, a piece jumped out of the pan and landed on the stone floor by my feet.

It would have been impolite to ignore it, and of course, no one else would have eaten it, so I gave it a few seconds to cool and then gobbled it down. Delicious.

Lila turned her attention to a stack of bread and began shoving it into a toaster. "I should have turned them away. If they'd gone to the hospital, they wouldn't have been trapped here, and Doctor Simister wouldn't have been hit by the beam. I know it was an accident."

"But you wanted to help," I said. "And for all we know, the hospital may be closed. In these extreme conditions, staff may not have been able to get in, or they may be overwhelmed by casualties."

Lila didn't appear to have heard me. "I need to toughen up. I'm a business owner. I can't take pity on a couple of passersby. Did you notice, last night, Doctor Simister made no mention of paying to stay while his wife recovered? And I expect they'd have wanted feeding, too. They tore through the buffet like they hadn't eaten in days."

"I'm sure he'd have paid you for your generosity," I said.

"My parents always called me gullible. It's got to change, or I'll never make this place a success." Lila thumped down the spatula. "Maybe I never will. Mrs. Simister is right. The second the locals hear about someone dying in the dining room, they'll start a rumor the place is haunted, or cursed, or worse!"

"Well, it is already haunted. And Willow is a charming ghost. That's an attraction, rather than a problem."

Lila viciously buttered the toast. "I won't let anyone accuse me of killing Doctor Simister. I am sorry this happened, but I wish he'd gotten squashed under a beam somewhere else." She glanced at me. "Make yourself useful and gather everyone for breakfast. Otherwise, this food will go to waste."

I left a grumbling Lila as she continued to stab the toast. As I headed into the corridor, Cythera and Finn were carrying Doctor Simister's body out of the dining room.

Finn nodded a greeting. "We're putting him in the cellar. It's cooler down there, and people will be less freaked out if they aren't concerned about stumbling over a corpse."

"Good thinking. When you're done, wash your hands then join us for breakfast," I said. "Lila's making bacon sandwiches."

He grinned. "Will do."

Five minutes later, everyone was in the guest sitting room. Nobody had wanted to eat their breakfast in the dining room, since Doctor Simister had just vacated the area. So, we sat with plates balanced on our laps or beside us and mugs of tea and coffee on the small table in the middle of the room. It was a subdued group, and I could tell by looking at everyone's faces there'd been little sleep.

"Has anyone tried to get out this morning?" Gaian asked.

"We're still trapped," I replied. "The inn wants us to stay a while longer."

"Perhaps it wants you to solve the murder." Gaian eyeballed Finn coldly as he bit into a bacon sandwich and grease dripped out of it.

"Murder!" Mrs. Simister exclaimed. "Why are we talking about murder?"

"Juno is talking about it. It's all she's been talking about." Gaian raised his eyebrows at me. "Why don't you share your thoughts? Or are you content to gossip behind people's backs with Zandra?"

"Hold on now," Finn said around a mouthful of sandwich. "We don't know for certain what happened last night."

"I knew it! I knew something bad happened to Idris." Mrs. Simister twisted in her seat to face Lila. "What do you know about this?"

"I'm not having this conversation again," Lila said. "You've already accused me of harming your husband. I didn't know him. I had no reason to want him dead. I brought you into the inn out of the kindness of my heart because you were injured. How was I to know you'd show up? Or did I have a plan up my sleeve that the next two strangers to walk through my door would be my victims? Be rational."

"Juno thinks you're a killer!" Mrs. Simister said.

"Not exactly." I resisted the urge to attack Gaian with my murder mittens for throwing me under the suspect bus and stirring the tension between Lila and Mrs. Simister.

"Then explain yourself," Lila said. "Do you think I had something to do with what happened to Doctor Simister?"

I looked at Zandra, and she nodded at me to go ahead. "I have concerns about his death. After Doctor Simister died, I looked at the beam. There were unusual markings on the end. They suggest someone cut the wood, which would have weakened the beam."

Lila shook her head. "I'd know if anyone had tampered with the beams. And it's not something anyone could easily do. It's no easy task to get up to the ceiling and work on them. The builders used scaffolding."

"You'd be able to get to them on a ladder," Gaian said. "Or if someone knew the right spells, they could have damaged the beam without touching it."

"They were in good condition," Lila said. "And the building inspector signed off on everything. He'd never have done that if there was a problem with the work."

"Maybe you tampered with the beam after he'd done his inspection," Mrs. Simister said.

Lila closed her eyes and let out a sigh. "Fine. It was me. I came up with the dastardly plan to murder a man I'd never met using an almost impossible weapon. Put me away, angels. I did it."

"There's no need to be sarcastic," Mrs. Simister snapped. "But it makes sense it was you. You had time to tinker."

"I've also inspected the beam," Cythera said. "The markings are consistent with cuts. It's also possible magic was used to achieve the same effect."

Lila sat back in her seat and crossed her arms over her chest. "Not by me."

"Everyone was in the dining room when the beam fell," I said. "And we all have magic."

"So, we're all suspects?" Lila said.

"Maybe Doctor Simister wasn't the target," Zandra said. "We were all moving around, getting food, and chatting. And the lights went out just before the beam fell. Perhaps the intended victim moved, and Doctor Simister took their place."

"You think someone is still vulnerable?" Lila asked. "Whoever did this may go after their actual victim next?"

No one spoke, and everyone looked unhappy. And I lost my appetite, despite the alluring bacon smell. If we stayed here much longer, would my wonderful witch be at risk from this killer with a flair for using odd murder weapons?

Chapter 7

Gathering evidence

After our tense breakfast and the discussion over the possibility the killer may strike again, no one felt much like eating. The group separated, but I remained with Zandra, Finn, Cythera, and Sage in the sitting room. Sorcha and Gaian wandered off together. Mrs. Simister went to lie down. Lila headed into the kitchen to clean up after breakfast, and Vorana took Ember for a bath after he got bacon grease on his fur. Willow was nowhere to be seen.

"We need a plan of action," I said. "Whatever is going on, we have to get to the bottom of it. We can all agree that the beam was tampered with."

Cythera looked at her watch. "We focus on getting out or making contact with the outside world so someone can rescue us."

"We've tried the doors and windows already this morning," Zandra said. "I got a shock from all of them when I attempted to get out. And no one is outside while the weather is this terrible, so we can't get anyone to see we're stuck in here."

"There must be a weakness to the spell that's keeping us trapped," Cythera said.

"We won't give up on trying to get out," I said. "But while we're in here, we may as well speak to everyone and see what happened with that beam."

Cythera pursed her lips and checked her watch once more.

"Is there somewhere you need to be?" I asked.

"I have a dress fitting in half an hour."

"That's hardly mission-critical," I said. "Your dressmaker will understand you've had to postpone because you're trapped in a haunted inn with a dead body in the cellar, a killer on the loose, and murder suspects that need interviewing."

"Mind your business." Cythera's words were so sharp, they almost flayed me.

"Of course. Just because I no longer wear clothing, I still appreciate a well-tailored outfit," I said.

"When have you ever worn clothing?" Zandra said. "You didn't speak to me for days when I suggested I get you some cute winter sweaters when it got cold."

I glanced at her and twitched my booping snooter. "Let's lay out the suspects and go from there."

"I'll lay out the suspects. After all, I have decades of experience dealing with troublemakers," Cythera snapped.

"Then the stage is yours." I settled next to Zandra on the couch.

Cythera took a moment, smoothing her hands over her white pants and tugging down the bottom of her shirt. "Lila Mingler-Mist is known to none of us. She should be our initial focus."

"She's responsible for the building's integrity," I said. "And as Mrs. Simister pointed out during their disagreement, she had the most access to the beam. And Lila's more upset about the possibility her business will fail because of Doctor Simister's death than what happened to him."

"She didn't know Doctor Simister, did she?" Sage said from her comfy resting place on a plump blue cushion.

"None of us knew him," Finn said.

Sage grunted. "So, it makes sense Lila would be shocked about what happened, but she wouldn't grieve a stranger."

"But Lila is still a murder suspect," I said. "And we only have everyone's word that they don't know the Simisters."

"Assuming there's even been a murder." Cythera's glare was full of warning that I was overstepping.

"It's an assumption I'm happy to run with. And you said someone had tampered with the beam."

"Possibly tampered with. Then we have the resident ghost, Willow," Cythera said. "I've barely spoken to her. She never stays in one room for long. Is anyone aware of her abilities?"

"I've not tested her power. Willow said she didn't have much magical talent, but she seems able to come and go at will, so she has some ability," I said. "She's anxious about something, but Willow is on our side."

"None of us know anything about Willow," Cythera said. "If I had access to the office, we could see if there's anything in the archives. A criminal record, maybe."

"How would Willow know Doctor Simister since she's so old?" Finn said.

"She doesn't. The couple has no connections here," I said. "I checked with Mrs. Simister, and Idris has never done business in Crimson Cove, and they have no friends in the area, so it's unlikely his path would have crossed with Willow's. And she can't leave the inn, so they wouldn't have met outside."

"Willow is still a suspect in this possible murder. Then we have Mrs. Gwendolyn Simister," Cythera said. "We know little about her, too."

"Just like Lila, she's a stranger, but she's distraught over her husband's death. It would be difficult to fake such emotion," I said.

"But not impossible," Cythera said. "Murderers are effective at being deceitful. It's how they get away with their crimes."

"Not when you're around." I hid my smiling face under Zandra's hand.

"Mrs. Simister was fortunate not to be crushed by that beam too," Finn said. "She went to the buffet with her husband just before the lights went out."

"Was it fortunate?" Sage asked. "Or was it because she knew what was about to happen and got out of the way?"

"Mrs. Simister doesn't strike me as a powerful magic user," Cythera said.

"She's admitted she's not. Old age has not been kind to her power," I said. "And when she attempted to get out of the inn this morning, she was injured. The magic damaged her hand and turned it green.

And when she threw a spell at Lila, her aim was terrible. I doubt the spell had much malice or power in it."

"But she must remain a suspect," Cythera said. "Perhaps not the prime suspect, though."

No one disagreed with her logic.

"Then there's all of us," Sage said. "We were in the dining room when it happened. And we're powerful magic users."

Cythera huffed out a breath. "We need to focus on the strangers, not the people we know."

"I don't think any of us in this room should be in the frame as suspects," I said.

"Nor Vorana," Sage said. "My witch is innocent."

Again, no one disagreed. We all knew and loved Vorana.

I glanced at the closed door. "However, I'm wondering about Gaian. He's not been in Crimson Cove long, and ever since he arrived, he's caused trouble."

"He's more bluster than bite. He acts like a big bad magic using maverick," Finn said, "but talk to him one-on-one and he's decent enough. And Sorcha wouldn't pick an idiot to date."

"Sometimes, love is blind," I said. "Sadly, that's the case with Gaian and Sorcha. You must have noticed how much she's changed since he showed up. He has an unhealthy amount of influence over her."

"I've only noticed changes at the café," Cythera said. "But we're watching his gang, especially since they've made Crimson Cove their base. Nothing has caused me any concern."

"They're ruffling feathers among the locals," I said. "We were all there when Gaian messed with Remus's festival."

"Why would Gaian want to kill Doctor Simister?" Finn said. "What's his motive? He didn't seem keen on staying long when he arrived last night."

I had no answer, but I was certain that was because I didn't have all the clues, not because Gaian was innocent.

"He's another possibility. But not my prime target," Cythera said. "Is that it?"

I looked around the group, not looking forward to making my next statement. "As reluctant as I am to throw this particular name into the suspect ring, we should also consider Sorcha."

"No way," Zandra said. "I get she's different now she's in a relationship with Gaian, but she's not a killer. Sorcha takes care of people. If Doctor Simister and his wife had shown up at her café, she'd have let them in and helped them, just like Lila did."

"Would she? The café is more Gaian's than hers anymore, and he doesn't let people in if they don't agree with his principles."

"We can't put Sorcha on the suspect list," Finn said. "I've known her for ages, and she's never triggered any alarms."

"She's never dated an idiot with aspirations to grandeur he doesn't deserve," I said. "He's turned her against her friends and ruined the café."

Sage nodded. "Vorana's devastated Sorcha has stopped talking to her. They had a couple of disagreements over Gaian, and that was it. Sorcha shut her out. She's definitely changed for the worse."

"It doesn't bring me joy to include Sorcha. As soon as possible, we can discount her," I said. "But because of her association with Gaian, she must be a suspect. Even if only to be considered as his accomplice."

"Very well," Cythera said. "That's covered everyone."

"No, it hasn't," Sage said.

Cythera glanced at Sage. "Who did I miss?"

"Ember Dreamscape."

"That adorable kitten Vorana's taken in?" Cythera tilted her head. "Why should he be a suspect?"

"Because that adorable kitten is a nightmare hidden under a fluffy veil of innocence." Sage stood firm on her front paws. "He's devious, lies, and sneaks around, sticking his nose in places he shouldn't."

"You're sure?" Finn said. "He seems like a cutie."

"I know things about him you don't. He's a liar."

"You should share the full story, so people understand Ember is more than meets the eye," I said.

Sage lowered her head a fraction and took in several deep breaths. "It's my fault he's here. I realized I wasn't enough of a familiar to support Vorana. I'm slowing down, getting old, and my magic isn't always what it needs to be. So, I recruited a new familiar for her. All above board. I went to the Academy, requested the best they had in the next graduating class, and interviewed them. Ember stood out, so I gave him a trial. Big mistake."

"I've worked with Ember, and he's a capable young cat and immensely powerful. His invisibility magic is excellent, but he's too young to take on such responsibility," I said.

"He's devious," Sage said. "I made the mistake of letting him get a paw in the door and when he realized how amazing it was to live with Vorana, he muscled his way in. He lied to her about being abandoned, and of course, she has such a soft heart that she let him stay."

"Which is unfortunate for you," Cythera said, "but why would that make him kill Doctor Simister?"

"I'm telling you this because it's proof that you can't trust him. Maybe Doctor Simister recognized him and was about to blow his cover, or he said something that offended Ember."

"I'm not sure," Cythera said. "Ember spends most of his time sleeping in that papoose Vorana wears. Surely, she'd have felt something if he fired a spell to knock down the beam."

"I've never met a more devious, sly little monster. Ember uses his good looks and fake charm to get what he wants." Sage stomped a paw. "And he's been creeping around this place. I found his muddy paw prints upstairs."

"Let's put him on the suspect list," I said before Cythera could protest. "Just to ensure we've missed nothing important."

Cythera arched an eyebrow but didn't argue any further.

"So, we have our suspects, but what about motives?" Finn said. "None of us knew Doctor Simister."

"I didn't recognize them," Cythera said. "But perhaps the suspects we don't know so well have met him before and are concealing that fact."

"Which means we focus on Lila and Mrs. Simister," Zandra said.

"Mrs. Simister is upset her husband is dead, but the killer often knows their victim, so it makes sense it could have been her," Finn said. "We can't check their backgrounds while we're in here, but it's possible their marriage had a violent past. Maybe reports have been filed about arguments."

"We must include Gaian, too," I said. "None of us know much about him."

"I know enough from the background checks my angels have run," Cythera said.

"If Gaian is on the list, then Ember needs to be made a priority, too," Sage said. "You don't know him like I do. I've been sleeping with one eye open since he moved into the house."

No one seemed to think that was an excellent idea, but Sage had a thunderous expression on her face, so there were no objections.

"We've already spoken to Mrs. Simister," I said. "We talked this morning and found no reason she wanted her husband dead."

"I'm sure you used the proper tactics to thoroughly question a murder suspect without causing alarm," Cythera said.

My hackles rose. Cythera always underappreciated me and Zandra. "I've seen enough of your interviews to know how to do things properly."

"Did she say anything to make you concerned about her?" Finn said.

"No. Mrs. Simister is mainly angry and grief-stricken," I said. "She was with her husband a long time. Over fifty years."

"If they didn't get along, she'll be glad he's dead. Maybe she saw this trip as an excuse to get rid of him," Zandra said.

I considered this possibility. "Mrs. Simister saw the crazy weather and magic and figured his death would be linked to that. Not her deep loathing of a man she's been with fifty years who eats with his mouth open and probably snores like a warthog. It's a theory worth pursuing."

"Love can quickly turn to hate," Finn said. "We'll need to handle her carefully, though."

"We'll tackle Mrs. Simister this morning," Cythera said. "Make sure you missed nothing."

"Who do you want us to talk to?" I asked, refusing to rise to Cythera's rudeness.

She didn't respond.

"Boss, we need help here. Zandra and Juno will do a good job. And without backup from the office, we're limited in what we can achieve if we tackle this on our own." Finn gave a slight shrug as he caught my eye.

Cythera's gaze went to the window. "Fine. But keep your questioning casual, and any information you find, bring it to me and Finn. You may speak to Lila."

"We can do that," I said. Although I had another target in mind to begin with.

"I'll keep watch on Ember," Sage said. "Make sure he's not doing anything sly, like figuring out how to slay his next victim."

"Excellent idea," I said. "Perhaps you could join him in the bath while he turns a rubber duck into a lethal weapon."

Sage hissed at me.

"Everyone get to work," Cythera said. "We'll meet here in two hours for an update."

I waited until Finn, Cythera, and Sage had left the room before turning to Zandra. "Before we speak to Lila, there's a certain ghost I'd like a word with."

Chapter 8

Ghostly gossip

"There she is!" I'd been searching for Willow with Zandra for twenty minutes. It was never easy to find a ghost who didn't want to be found.

Willow swirled back and forth at the bottom of a set of wooden steps that led to an attic hatch in the ceiling.

"Go gently with her," Zandra cautioned. "She spooks easily. We don't want her to vanish again before we question her."

I trotted ahead of Zandra. "Greetings! I'm glad we found you."

Willow slowed for a second, her gaze anxious as it dropped to mine. "I keep hearing things."

I stopped in front of her. "What kind of things?"

"Noises from the attic. Scratching and rustling sounds. I don't like it."

Zandra studied the closed hatch. "Maybe this place has rodents. They love old buildings. Lots of holes to sneak in through. Hey! Maybe they damaged the beam in the dining room by gnawing on it."

"How would they do that?" I asked. "They couldn't have scurried up the wall and gnawed on the beam while suspended by their ratty paws."

Zandra pointed at the attic hatch. "They did it from overhead. There are probably crawl spaces between the floors and ceilings. Rats can squish into any tiny space they like. They're determined little critters. Sharp teeth, too."

"Rats!" Willow said. "Do you really think it's rats up there? I don't like them. They're big and mean. And they leave droppings everywhere."

"We're getting ahead of ourselves," I said. "It may not be rodents. Perhaps it's another friendly ghost looking for a buddy."

Willow glowered at me. "No! This is my inn. I'm the only ghost allowed to live here."

"But you got little choice in that, did you?" I said. "Do you remember much about the person who trapped you here?"

Willow kept her gaze on the ceiling. "I thought I was doing a good deed by calling out that creep."

"What did you do?" Zandra asked.

"The man who ran the place enjoyed harassing his female servants. He was the boss, so there was little anyone could do when he pressed his unwanted attentions on them. So, I taught him a lesson. I wanted him to see he didn't have all the power."

"That was why he hexed you?" I said.

Willow nodded. "He was a petty man. And I stole from him, not because I needed the money, but to make him realize he wasn't invulnerable, and he needed to watch his back. He should look after his servants, not exploit them. He caught me. I expected to be punished, but I never expected this." She lifted a wispy arm.

"Have you tried to break the hex?" I asked as a soft scratching came from overhead.

"Of course! And others have tried to help me, too. Perhaps you'll be the one to succeed." Willow's eyes glinted with optimism.

"Let's hope so," I said. "But if my efforts fail, you'll have lots of company now the inn is almost open for business."

"I don't like company." Willow's smile faded. "I have nothing against Lila, though. And she doesn't mind me being here. Not that she could do much about it if she did. It's fun to see a woman in charge after so many years of my creepy boss getting to do whatever he liked."

"Did you watch the renovations while they were going on?" Zandra asked.

"Sometimes. It got too noisy and crowded, though, so I'd leave. Well, I got to go two steps into the yard. I spent a lot of time out there when they were cutting tiles. It was so noisy."

"Did you see Lila have any trouble with the builders?" I said. "Maybe she was asking them not to finish certain jobs or to do things on the cheap."

Willow stopped swirling around and looked at me. "You'll have to ask her. I like Lila. Some people have no patience with ghosts, but she sits with me and has a mug of coffee some afternoons. We don't talk about anything in particular, but she's nice."

"It must feel good to have a friend," I said. "But if you know anything about the renovations not going as planned, you need to tell us. We have to find out what happened to Doctor Simister."

Willow went quiet for a few seconds, her teeth gnawing at her lower lip. "What do you think happened to him?"

"That's what we're investigating. Was it an accident, or did someone do this deliberately? And if they did, we're all trapped in here with a killer." I glanced at Zandra. Willow was nervous about something.

"I could show you a secret. It might help you. But I don't want to get Lila in trouble." Willow's voice was almost a whisper.

"Anything. We need evidence before we make our next move," Zandra said.

Willow led us to an empty, unfinished guest bedroom and pointed at an old cabinet pushed against the wall.

Zandra shoved the cabinet to one side, revealing a wall covered in damp and black mold. "Are all the rooms like this?"

"Not all of them. This is the worst. Lila was running out of money. She couldn't afford to have the rooms properly sealed." Willow sighed. "The damp is coming from the outside. She was supposed to have external weatherproofing put on the building, but she didn't have the funds to complete the job, so she asked the builders to do a basic whitewash and said she'd get around to it later."

"Mold can make people sick," I said. "If Lila skimped on this, it's possible she didn't have the work done on the beams."

"Lila said an inspector signed off on the job," Zandra said. "She wouldn't be allowed to open without the proper permits."

"Inspectors can be bribed or things get overlooked. And a cursory glance at the beams wouldn't have revealed any fault," I said.

"If Lila was racking up debts and unable to pay her builders, they could have left some jobs unfinished. She didn't necessarily know the beam would fall on anyone."

"But that doesn't explain the gouge marks on the fallen beam," I said. "They were made deliberately to weaken it."

We all held our breaths as scratching and rustling noises came from overhead.

"Those sound like big rats," Zandra said. "Maybe they chewed the beam and made those marks. The rats are responsible for squashing Doctor Simister."

"We can hardly charge rats with murder," I said. "As oddly charming an idea it is that we have murderous rats and not a murderous magic user to deal with, I don't think that's the line of inquiry we should pursue."

Zandra gestured with her chin to the attic hatch. "Should we take a look? See what type of critter we're sharing the inn with?"

"You stay here. I'll deal with any rats if they're up there." I put a paw on the bottom rung of the wooden steps.

"Be careful!" Willow said. "In my time, rats carried the Black Death. I was always terrified of them. I'd put mint and sage by my bedroom door so they wouldn't creep in. They don't like those scents."

"I'll come with you." Zandra set one foot on the wooden staircase, when there was a cry for help from Gaian.

Rushing back down the main stairs, all thoughts of gnawing attic rats forgotten, we discovered two trails of blood leading from the dining room into the guest sitting room.

"Who's been hurt?" Zandra's head whipped from side to side as she inspected the confusing scene.

Willow had followed us down the stairs. She took one look at the chaos and vanished.

"It's Cythera and Finn!" Sorcha was tugging on the door leading into the sitting room, Gaian assisting her. "We came out of the kitchen to see them being pulled along the floor. They were out cold."

"Pulled by what?" I said. "Who attacked them? How badly injured are they?"

"We've no idea," Gaian said.

"You must have seen who hurt them," I said.

"They were being dragged by an invisible force." Sorcha leaned her shoulder against the door. "I can't get into this room."

"We'll try." I jumped on Zandra's shoulder, and we connected our magic. She held out her hands and pressed them against the door. A spell exploded from her palms. It ricocheted back and knocked her off her feet, sending us tumbling to the floor.

"Yeah, I should have warned you about that," Gaian said. "I tried an unlock spell and got a burned arm." He exposed his injured wrist. "Finn and Cythera are locked inside, and they're not getting out."

I rolled onto my paws and checked if Zandra was okay. She struggled to her feet and rubbed her chest where the spell had whacked into her.

"Finn. Cythera. Can you hear us?" I asked, shaking out my fur.

There was no reply.

"We haven't heard a sound from them," Sorcha said. "We heard them yelling, and then it went quiet."

"They must be badly injured." I glanced at the blood on the floor.

"Are they dead?" Mrs. Simister stood in the dining room doorway, her face pale.

A muffled groan came from the other side of the locked door. It sounded like Finn.

"Finn! Say something. How badly are you injured?" I asked.

There were a few seconds of silence, and then a soft shuffling grew closer to the door. "I'm alive. Feel terrible, though. The back of my head is killing me."

I breathed a sigh of relief. "And Cythera?"

"Unconscious but breathing."

"What happened?" Zandra pressed her ear against the door.

"We were sitting at the table in the dining room, speaking to Mrs. Simister, and then I got this pain in the back of my head. Then I was moving. Something knocked me down and dragged me by my ankles. I couldn't see what it was." Finn's voice was groggy and his words slurred.

"Something in this place doesn't want its secrets revealed," Gaian said. "The angels were digging into trouble, and this is what happens."

I hissed softly. No one hurt my friends and got away with it. We had to get to the bottom of this before more people were injured or worse. "Gaian and Sorcha, stay by the door. Keep trying to get it open."

Gaian scowled at me. "I'm not risking Sorcha's safety by using more magic. It's too risky."

"Don't use magic, then. Try the traditional way. Get an axe, or pry the hinges off. Be inventive! Finn and Cythera need to get out of there."

"We'll help," Sorcha said. "We'll stay and watch over them and see what we can do about getting the door open."

I nodded my appreciation. "We need to talk to Mrs. Simister," I said to Zandra.

She scooped me up and settled me back on her shoulder, then we stalked to where Mrs. Simister stood. We entered the dining room and discovered two chairs knocked over. There was also a large metal candlestick on the floor.

"Is this what hit Finn and Cythera?" Zandra asked Mrs. Simister as she inspected the candlestick.

She nodded and staggered to a seat. "It shot off the mantle above the fireplace. See, there's its pair. At first, I couldn't believe what I was seeing. It hit Cythera and then Finn. It was so fast that I didn't have a chance to warn them to duck."

We joined her, righting the chairs before sitting.

"Then what happened?" I asked.

"A foul-smelling green fog smothered us, and I couldn't see either of them. But I could hear them. They were fighting something, yelling, and things were being knocked over."

"Were you hurt when this invisible force attacked?" Zandra said.

Mrs. Simister shook her head. "The green fog didn't hurt me. Maybe it was meant to confuse me, so I couldn't help them."

"What were you talking about when they were attacked?" I asked.

Mrs. Simister's hands were clasped in her lap, but I could see they were shaking. "They were asking me about Idris. We were talking about our visit and if he knew anyone in the area." A tear trickled down her cheek. "This terrible inn is full of darkness. We must leave before anyone else dies."

I looked at the window. "No one is going anywhere."

"This place wants us as guests for a while longer." Gaian stood by the open door, leaning against the door jamb.

"You're supposed to be getting the angels free," I said.

"Sorcha's looking for tools. We're going to pry the hinges out. Although what good it'll do us, I don't know. If this inn is determined to keep us here, we can try all we like, but nothing will work."

I didn't think there was any malevolence in the fabric of the building, but there was someone in here who had a dark heart and devious motives. And with my wonderful witch by my side, I intended to find out who it was.

Chapter 9

Mystery muddle

Sorcha, and to some degree, Gaian, worked for hours, trying to get the guest sitting room door open. The hinges wouldn't budge, and any attempts to break through with an axe were met with fierce magical resistance that meant everyone was reluctant to keep trying for fear of being burned or bitten.

Lila, Vorana, Ember, Sage, and Willow had joined us, although Willow kept flitting away, an anxious expression on her face.

"We may have to admit defeat," I said through the door to Finn, as Gaian tossed down a bent screwdriver.

"We're okay in here for now. Cythera's breathing is even, and I'm feeling better. I've healed the worst of my injury. I still have a headache, though."

"We'll keep looking for a way to get you free," I said. "And we'll keep you updated about the investigation. Once we know who's behind this, we'll force them to let you out."

"When Cythera wakes, I'm sure she'll appreciate that," Finn said. "So will I. We'll settle in and rest. I know we can rely on you."

"Gaian and I will guard the room," Sorcha said. "We can take shifts and make sure you're never left alone in case this entity comes back for you."

"Thanks. I'm not in a fighting mood while my head's pounding like it's been kicked by a dragon a few dozen times."

"If anyone's hungry, I've made sandwiches," Lila said. "I'll leave them in the kitchen, so you can help yourselves whenever you want a snack."

"I could eat," Gaian said.

Sorcha rested against the door. "I'll stay here."

"You sure? I hate leaving you."

She smiled. "Bring me back a plate."

"Me too," Finn called out. "Oh! Wait! I can't get to the food. This is so unfair."

"I usually leave a few snacks and bottles of water in the desk drawers," Lila said. "They'll keep you going until we figure this out."

"I'll take a look."

"And I'll make a start on our evening meal." Lila headed toward the kitchen. "I know it's early, but I'd rather keep busy than pace around worrying about how we're supposed to get out or what's going to happen next to make sure my inn never gets an official opening."

"I could do with a rest," Mrs. Simister said. "I'm sorry. I've been no use in helping to get the angels free. I'm a burden."

"You're not." Vorana walked over and guided Mrs. Simister to the bottom of the stairs. "You've got a lot on your plate. You rest. Ember, help Mrs. Simister up the stairs and into bed. Make sure she's comfortable."

He hopped out of his papoose, shook his freshly washed fur, and nodded before trotting along beside Mrs. Simister, who held onto the rail as she pulled herself up the stairs.

"We need to talk," I whispered to Vorana and Sage when she re-joined us.

"Sure. About what?"

I glanced at Sorcha to make sure she wasn't paying us any attention, but her gaze was on the sitting room door as she spoke to Finn. "Not here. Let's go to the dining room, where we can talk without being overheard."

We headed into the dining room, but before Zandra eased the door closed, I dashed back out, an urge for a sandwich getting the better of me.

I paused in the kitchen doorway. Gaian and Lila were talking. Or more like bickering. They stood close, and Gaian had hold of Lila's left arm. His brow was furrowed and his words low, so I couldn't hear what he said. Lila didn't look happy, but then she grinned and shoved him.

He scowled at her and made to grab her arm again, but she stepped back, shaking her head. Was there something going on between them?

"Juno! What are you doing?" Zandra whispered from the dining room doorway.

I glanced over my shoulder then looked back at Lila and Gaian. He was heading my way, so I hurried away and snuck into the dining room.

"Where'd you go?" Zandra said.

"I wanted a sandwich then changed my mind." I was uncertain what to make of Gaian and Lila's conversation. I'd need to mull it over before drawing conclusions. If he was cheating on Sorcha with Lila, I'd skin him alive, then obliterate him, then magic back the pieces and do it all over again. Several times. No one cheated on Sorcha.

I waited until we were all seated before focusing on the current issue. "Someone in this place is behind this mess."

"And they don't want the truth to come out," Zandra said.

I nodded. "Finn and Cythera were asking about Doctor Simister's death when they got attacked and removed from assisting us with this investigation. That leaves few people in here I completely trust," I said. "You and Sage are two of them. My wonderful witch goes without saying. But that's it."

Vorana glanced at the closed door. "What about Sorcha? Shouldn't we include her?"

"We can't rely on Sorcha. Not while she's so enamored with Gaian."

Vorana's eyebrows lifted. "You think he's behind the attack on the angels?"

"I don't like him. And I don't trust him."

"What about me? You can trust me!" Ember popped into view, surrounded by a shimmer of sparkling magic.

Sage snarled and launched at him. She latched her murder mittens around his head and rolled him over. He hissed and kicked her belly. Sage bit into one of his ears, making him squeak.

"Stop that!" Vorana strode over and lifted Sage off of Ember. "What's he ever done to you?"

"He snuck in! He was supposed to be helping Mrs. Simister." Sage bared her yellowed teeth and hissed at him again. "He can't be trusted, either. He must leave."

"I didn't sneak in! Well, maybe I did, but I wanted to show everyone how amazing my invisibility magic is." Ember was already on his paws and licking his fur back into place.

Sage struggled in Vorana's grasp, squirming to get free and continue her attack.

"Sage, this isn't like you." Vorana held her tight. "I thought you liked Ember."

Sage blasted a spell from her paw, and it whacked Ember in the butt. "How can you expect me to like anything so deceitful?"

"What are you talking about? He's been nothing but sweet to you since he moved in."

"Sage, I know you're not Ember's biggest fan," I said, "but he could be useful. His advanced invisibility magic gives him an opportunity to listen to conversations people don't want us to overhear."

"It also gives him the opportunity to sneak about and kill people," Sage said. "Have you thought about that? Maybe he attacked the angels. He can become invisible with the click of a paw."

"Why would Ember do such a thing?" Vorana said. "Sage, I'm disappointed in you."

"I like the angels," Ember said. "They're the good guys. I'd never hurt them."

"He can't be here," Sage said. "We don't trust him. He's a suspect too."

"You think he hurt Doctor Simister?" Vorana said. "Why? You didn't know Doctor Simister, did you, Ember?"

"I've never met him before. And I'd never hurt him. Sage isn't making any sense." A smug expression flashed across his face but then vanished. "I don't blame Sage for saying such hurtful things to me. She's old and has been under a lot of stress recently."

"Ever since you moved in," Sage said on a snarl.

Vorana placed Sage on the floor. "Behave! No more jumping on Ember. Come here, sweetie. Let me make sure your ear didn't get too badly bitten."

Ember's expression was smug again as Vorana lifted him onto her lap as she crouched and examined him.

I sidled over to Sage and nudged her. "I know you hate that kitten, but we need all the help we can get. Maybe Ember should be included."

She speared me with a vicious glare. "You can't seriously want him in this group."

"We'll only give him easy tasks. Listening into conversations, that sort of thing. And if he's with us, you can watch over him more easily."

"What if he's the killer?" Sage said. "He'll know what we're planning and ruin it."

"I heard that." Vorana settled Ember into his papoose. "Ember is kind-hearted and sweet. He wouldn't do anything so nasty as killing a person. I'm ashamed of you for even thinking that, Sage."

Sage lowered her head, while Ember's smugness grew.

I patted my friend's side. "As I was saying, we must move fast with this mystery. The fact the angels got injured when asking questions means whoever is behind this is determined to keep their identity secret."

"And whoever injured Finn and Cythera most likely killed Doctor Simister," Zandra said. "If we can find that person, we find the killer."

I nodded. "Where was everyone when the angels were attacked? We were upstairs with Willow and Sage."

"I was bathing Ember," Vorana said.

"What about Gaian and Sorcha?" I asked.

"In the dining room with Mrs. Simister?" Zandra said.

"No, she was with Finn and Cythera." Vorana sighed. "Sorcha isn't involved in this, and she'd have nothing to do with Gaian if she thought he was a killer."

"We still need to check where they were," I said. "Lila?"

Zandra shrugged. "She spends a lot of time in the kitchen."

"She said she came out of the kitchen," Sage said. "That's close enough to the dining room to throw a spell to injure the angels."

"Lila's not powerful, though," I said. "I get a tingly vibe when I'm around someone who has strong magic. I experienced it the first time I met my witch. I got chills."

Zandra smirked. "If Lila is involved, we still have to figure out why she did it."

I put the suspects in their respective places and added the innocent parties around them. "Is Gaian behind this? I keep returning to him as the prime suspect."

"Or Mrs. Simister," Vorana said. "She could have done something to Finn and Cythera when they questioned her. No one would have seen if she cast a spell because it was just the three of them in the dining room."

"But why?" Zandra said. "And where did she get the magic? When I saw her cast a spell, it fizzled away without making an impact. You need a heap of power to take down two angels."

"There's no motive for anyone to kill Doctor Simister," I said. "Not that we've uncovered. But someone did it, and they're working hard to stop questions being asked."

"Does anyone know how powerful Willow is?" Vorana asked.

"She must be strong," Ember said. "She keeps saying she's been here a long time. Ghosts that lack a regular energy source fade, and from what I've heard, this place has been empty for ages. They can't recharge on thin air."

"Maybe Willow recently got a boost of power," Vorana said. "This place has been busy with builders and inspectors, and Lila's been coming and going for months. Willow could have drawn from their energy to regenerate."

"She's good at disappearing and popping up unexpectedly," Ember said.

"Just like you," Sage grumbled.

"But she also doesn't know the Simisters," I said. "And Willow was upstairs with us when Finn and Cythera were injured." I let the twisty possibilities drift around my mind. "Someone is hiding the reason they're here. We need to dig deeper and find out what secrets people are keeping."

A pile of soot landed in the cold chimney hearth. Several white feathers followed.

Vorana hurried to the chimney breast. "Has a bird gotten caught? We can't let the poor thing remain stuck, or it'll die of fright."

More white feathers appeared, and I grabbed one as it floated through the air. "This feather doesn't belong to a bird. This belongs to a—"

An enormous, soot-covered angel thudded into the hearth.

Chapter 10

Angel delight

"Who are you, and how did you break through the impossible-to-destroy magic barrier?" I stared at the grubby angel as he lay in the hearth, a stunned expression on his handsome face. He was movie star good-looking, with sandy brown hair and eyes that were more green than typical angel blue.

He blinked several times but didn't move. "I'm Dimitri Stalinksi. Angel Force sent me. We've been trying to reach Cythera to get an update on the crisis."

"You've come to the right place." I eyed the chimney. "Is the barrier down? Can we leave?"

"Let me get you out of there." Zandra held out a hand and heaved Dimitri to his feet.

He staggered before righting himself. "Thanks. That was a journey I don't want to repeat anytime soon."

"The window still won't open." Vorana was attempting to lift a small window in the room under Sage's watchful gaze.

"You won't be able to get out," Dimitri said. "Half a dozen angels used their power to make a tiny crack in whatever is keeping you in here, and I forced my way through. We've been trying the door, but it won't budge. And we kept getting injured every time we used magic."

"Are the angels still outside?" I said. "Are they working on getting us free?"

He shook his head. "Haven't you seen how bad things are out there? We don't have a body to spare. Central Command has sent backup, but there aren't enough of us. The second I was in the chimney and gave them a thumbs-up, they flew off on other missions. We're overwhelmed with calls for help."

"There may still be time to escape," I said. "I'm small. I'll fit up that chimney. If you came down it, I can definitely go up."

"I wouldn't recommend it." Dimitri's expression grew worried. "Whatever magic is trapping you in here has a nasty flavor. I felt like I was being stabbed with a thousand tiny knives as I forced my way through. If I wasn't an angel, well, part angel, I may not have survived the fall."

"I'm as powerful as you. Maybe more so." I looked at Zandra. "Give me a boost. If I can get out, I can gather resources and free everyone."

"Are you sure?" She lifted me. "I don't want you getting injured."

"There's a chest full of powerful magic sitting in Vorana's basement. This is the perfect opportunity to use it. We've tried everything to get out from this side, and it's failed. It's time for a new plan."

"I advise extreme caution before attempting to use the chimney," Dimitri said. "It could kill you."

"Juno's smart. She knows what she's doing." Zandra pressed a kiss on my head. "Don't get yourself killed, or I'll never forgive you."

"I'd never do such a thing because that would mean leaving you."

Zandra positioned me underneath the open chimney. I looked up into an intense blackness that stank of smoke.

"Here we go." I added a bounce spell to my leap and made it ten feet up the chimney before finding a brick to grab and scramble up.

I was doing it! I was getting filthy, but this was our way out. Once I was free, I could —

Something hot and sharp dug into my side and shook me, whacking me against the rough brick. I clung to the inside of the chimney, but my claws wouldn't hold as something repeatedly slammed me against the roughhewn, blackened bricks.

I vaguely heard Zandra's voice echoing up the chimney shaft, but I couldn't respond. The pain in my side intensified, sending daggers of agony through me. I howled, and then I was falling, bumping against the side of the chimney on my way down, like a pinball in a machine.

A solid pair of hands caught me before I slammed into the hearth, and Zandra drew me against her chest. "I thought I told you not to get yourself killed."

I blinked soot out of my eyes, my side throbbing. "I'm still breathing. Just."

She held me close, and I could feel her rapid heartbeat. "Where are you hurt?"

"The spell hit my left side. It felt like a bite."

Zandra rested her hand over my side and pulsed out a powerful blast of healing magic, which wound around me like a heated blanket and soothed the pain.

"Is she okay?" Dimitri asked. "I did say it wasn't the wisest course of action. I'm an enormous angel, so I can withstand most kinds of twisted magic, but she's only a tiny familiar. You shouldn't have let her try."

"I make my own decisions," I murmured. At least, I think that was what I said. My ears still rang, and my vision was blurred and gritty.

"Juno will be fine," Zandra said. She made the introductions while she continued to heal me.

"I'm glad I could get in to help you. We almost gave up." Dimitri patted his chest. "Although I should be upfront with you all. I'm a recent graduate. I was with my training mentor when we got the alert that Crimson Cove was under attack by an unknown magical force. I've passed my exams, though, so I know the protocols."

"A rookie is here to save the day." I had my eyes closed but felt Zandra give me a gentle warning squeeze to cut back on the sass. "My apologies. All help is welcome."

"I'd like to talk to Cythera. We learned from some locals she was last seen coming in here. Is she still here?" Dimitri asked.

"She's here," Zandra said. "She's with another angel, too. Finn. But they were attacked while questioning suspects. They've been injured and are locked in a room. We've been unable to get them free."

"Suspects! Has a crime been committed?" Dimitri said.

"A murder." I opened my eyes. There was only one of Dimitri standing in front of me. That was progress. "Cythera and Finn were questioning the dead man's wife when an invisible force attacked them. They were hit with a candlestick and dragged into a room. Finn is conscious and healing, but Cythera has yet to wake."

Dimitri gulped and tugged at his dirty shirt. "I'd hoped Cythera would know what was going on. No one knows why Crimson Cove has been attacked."

"I may have answers for you." I gently nudged Zandra's hand away with my paw. I was feeling better now she'd healed me and was eager to continue the investigation. "But first, I need a bath. So do you. I'm not a fan of the tub, but I stink, and I'm not sure my fur will ever look the same again after that experience."

"I should speak to the other angels." Dimitri grimaced at his torn and filthy clothing. "But five minutes to freshen up would be okay. I want to look my best when I meet Cythera. She's my idol."

"You don't say? What an interesting choice of idol." I nudged Zandra with my head. "A sink of warm suds and a bar of soap is calling my name if you'd do the honors."

She kept me in her arms as she curtseyed. "Of course, your majesty."

While it took me less than three minutes to be bathed and enjoy a brisk rub down with a towel, Dimitri took twenty minutes to freshen up. He emerged from the guest bedroom we were using, squeaky clean and smelling of rose-scented shower gel. He wore a white bathrobe that was too small for him and exposed an impressive amount of toned thigh.

He looked at the robe, and a pink flush lit his cheeks. "I didn't want to wear my dirty clothes. Maybe I can get them cleaned while I'm here."

"I'm sure Lila, the owner, will help you," Zandra said.

Dimitri grabbed his bundle of clothing, then we left the bedroom and headed down the stairs to the guest sitting room.

Sorcha sat outside the door on a chair. Her eyes widened when she saw the new arrival. "I heard we had a visitor. Gaian saw you when you went upstairs. How did you get in?"

"This is Dimitri. He came down the chimney," I said.

"Who's Dimitri? Is the barrier down?" Finn asked. The door handle turned several times, but the door didn't open, and he cursed as magic must have nipped him with a warning.

"The barrier is still keeping us trapped," I said. "Dimitri's here to help." I made the introductions through the door.

"We're glad to have you here," Finn said. "What's going on outside?"

"We're figuring that out," Dimitri said. "I was sent in to get Cythera free. I didn't expect to find angels injured and trapped and someone dead."

"It's not how we planned on spending our time either," Finn said. "Juno and Zandra are leading the investigation into Doctor Simister's death. We work with them on some of our difficult cases."

Dimitri looked at us, surprise on his face. "You're experienced consultants?"

"The very best," I said. "It's why Angel Force relies on us so heavily. We're indispensable to them."

There was a chuckle from Finn. "Something like that. How's it all going?"

I glanced at Sorcha. "We have a shortlist of suspects. Lila and Mrs. Simister are on the list."

"That makes sense since we know the least about them."

"Did someone say my name?" Lila emerged from the kitchen. She stopped and stared at Dimitri. "And you are..."

"Dimitri has come to save the day," I said.

"I'll do my best." Dimitri shook Lila's hand. "I'm fresh out of graduate school, though."

"Well, all help is appreciated," Lila said. "Any idea how we can get out? Is the chimney an option?"

"No!" I said at the same time as Zandra.

"We're working on the problem," Dimitri said. "We've got all the spare angels we could gather in Crimson Cove to deal with the growing problems in town."

"We're aware things have been building for some time. Fights, bad weather, animals misbehaving. Anything else we've missed?" I asked.

"Everyone's magic seems unstable. People are fearful and angry, and there's a strange bubble of power around the town. We had trouble getting across the town lines. It took us hours to find a weakness, then it reformed behind us."

"You think it's the same kind of bubble that's trapped us in the inn?" Finn asked.

"I'm no expert, but it makes sense it would be connected." Dimitri massaged the back of his neck.

He seemed lost, so I gave him a boost of confidence. "If you didn't recognize the surname Crypt when the introductions were made, Zandra is one of the most powerful witches you'll ever have the privilege of meeting. I have a unique skill set, too. And although Cythera has sharp edges, she's a capable angel. And Finn is part demon. You're not alone."

"We're not that special," Zandra said. "We're a muddled bunch. Juno calls us her misfits."

"I know about the Crypt witches." Dimitri's eyes were wide as his gaze lingered on me. "You're powerful, too?"

"Don't underestimate me because I'm small and a perplexing chimney defeated me."

He nodded. "Understood. I'm glad of any help to solve this. I'm out of my depth. I was only nominated to come down the chimney because I was the smallest angel in the group."

I checked out his bulging biceps and bit my tongue.

"Is Cythera awake?" Dimitri said. "I was told to take instruction from her."

"Sorry, you're stuck with me," Finn said. "She's barely stirred since we were dragged in here. The others can fill you in. It might be easier than talking to a door."

"Oh! Right. I... sure. But let me know when Cythera is awake. My superior was very clear that she's in charge."

"Will do."

Lila glanced over her shoulder into the kitchen. "I was coming to say I've made afternoon snacks. Tea and cake if people are interested. Dimitri, you must join us. Perhaps we can figure out what to do now you're here. So far, we keep coming up against trouble and getting stuck."

"I'll do my best to assist." He held out his grubby ball of clothing. "Would you mind cleaning these? I got dirty coming down the chimney."

Lila took his clothes. "Of course. I'll serve in five minutes if everyone wants to go into the dining room."

We headed into the room and settled into seats. Ember was sent up to get Mrs. Simister, who came down, not looking like she'd had any sleep, and sat next to Lila, who was at the head of the table. Sorcha remained by the guest sitting room but was provided with a large plate of freshly made fruit cake and mini cheese scones.

The gathering was subdued, and while I picked at my cake, I stealthily watched Lila and Mrs. Simister. Their stilted, polite interactions suggested they were strangers. If Lila was behind killing Doctor Simister, I couldn't understand her motive.

Mrs. Simister pushed her fruit cake around the plate, using a napkin to dab at her eyes from time to time.

"Now we have help, it won't be long before we're free," I said to her. "Angel Force knows we're trapped. They won't leave us stranded."

She took a sip from her cup, her hands shaking. "Will the angels help me, though? The other two were questioning me as if they thought I was guilty of something."

"Cythera can be sharp. It's just her way. What questions did she ask you?" I said.

"She kept asking if my marriage was happy. Why wouldn't it be?"

"You'd been together a long time. It's natural you had disagreements over the decades. Did anything serious ever put a pin in your marital bliss?"

"Well, we had a few squabbles. And I've never hidden that, as we got older, our marriage became more of a friendship than a passionate love affair. We were comfortable, and we suited each other." Mrs. Simister dropped her fork onto the plate. "I'll be lost without him."

Lila reached over and touched Mrs. Simister's arm. "I am so sorry this happened. If there was a problem with the beam, maybe it was caused by the bad weather. I've been thinking about it, and the chimney stack was struck by lightning not long before you arrived. I went outside to see how badly it had been damaged, but I couldn't see clearly. Maybe the strike loosened the beam. I promise I wouldn't risk lives to save some money."

Mrs. Simister sniffed. "Maybe it wasn't your fault, but I sense something dark in this place. It's so cold in some of the rooms. Our room is icy."

"It's an old building, but I can turn up the heating this evening if that would help," Lila said. "There's no malevolence here, though. It's an old place with a few drafts."

"It's more than that. There's something nasty here. And it's still here. Which one of us will it come after next?" Mrs. Simister stifled a sob with her hand.

"Nothing will get you. Not now I'm here." Dimitri didn't look convinced by his own words.

"You don't need to worry about dark spirits," Gaian said, seated at the other end of the table. "They attach themselves to a particular person, usually someone with a cold heart and cruel thoughts. And you strike me as an honest, decent woman. Not the kind that would draw the interest of something unpleasant."

"You know a lot about dark spirits," I said. "Why would that be, since you're so intent on saving the world one carrot at a time?"

"I've been around the block, and I've learned a few things," Gaian said smoothly.

My hackles rose. "I can guarantee I've been around and seen things that would turn your hair white. You're not the expert here."

"And you are?"

Zandra cleared her throat, giving me a warning glance. "Lila, have you really sensed nothing odd in the inn since you've been here? These old places can attract distorted energies."

She shook her head. "No, nothing like that. There's just Willow, and she's usually sweet. She keeps to herself most of the time. I'm sure this was an accident. I've felt nothing troubling. No dark energy."

Mrs. Simister cried quietly, and the rest of us looked on uncomfortably.

My appetite dimmed as I puzzled over this twisty conundrum. What happened to Doctor Simister, and who attacked the angels?

I glanced at Dimitri. I had to hope our angel reinforcement would help put the pieces together. Although the way Dimitri fumbled with his scone and looked almost as unhappy as Mrs. Simister to be here, I had my doubts we were any further along with figuring this out.

Chapter 11

Curious clues

I rolled over and bumped into Zandra's back. After our miserable afternoon meal and an equally dismal dinner last night, no one had been in the mood for small talk, and it had been impossible to get any of the suspects alone to interrogate them, so we'd all had an early night.

I was back in the guest bedroom with Mrs. Simister, who'd taken the bed again. Since Finn and Cythera were trapped in the sitting room, Zandra and I had the luxury of the couch. It hadn't made for the most pleasant sleeping experience, but it was better than the floor.

Zandra grunted and shuffled around. I tilted my head as small scuffling sounds came from the attic. We still needed to investigate that rodent matter Willow was worried about.

"Are you awake?" Zandra said softly.

I stood, stretched, then hopped over her and landed by her face. I dabbed my booping snooter on her cheek. "Did you dream of a solution to this mystery?" I whispered, not wanting to rouse Mrs.

Simister, since she'd spent most of the night crying before falling silent just before dawn.

"I've no idea what's going on. Maybe everyone is paranoid and Doctor Simister wasn't killed. If lightning hit this building, the vibration could have dislodged the beam."

"What if Lila's not telling the truth but covering her tracks by claiming there was a lightning strike?" I asked.

"Or someone else is lying. Someone we're sharing a room with." Zandra's mouth was pressed to my ear and her voice low.

"I slept with one eye open. We had nothing to fear."

"I'm never scared when you're around." Zandra snuggled me against her chest for a few minutes. "I'd better get up and check on Finn and Cythera. Maybe Cythera's awake by now and has some idea of how to sort this out."

"There's a first time for everything."

Fifteen minutes later, and after Zandra had used the bathroom—as had I, after all, even a magical cat has essential needs to tend to—we left Mrs. Simister asleep and huddled under a pile of bedding and went down the stairs to the guest sitting room.

Sorcha was still sitting by the door. Her head was back and her mouth open as she slumbered. She jerked awake as we approached and blinked blearily. "Hey. Sorry, I didn't mean to nod off."

"Have you been here all night?" I asked.

Sorcha scratched her forehead and fluffed her hair. "Yeah. Gaian had a headache. I didn't want him getting ill by staying up all night."

"You were here all day, though," Zandra said. "You even ate your dinner by the door."

Sorcha's eyes narrowed. "I was happy to do it. Gaian needed to rest."

"So do you," I said.

Her gaze dropped to the floor. "Stop making a big deal out of it. I know none of you like Gaian, but it's not like he forced me to sit in this chair all night. I got up and walked around plenty of times. I even saw Dimitri a few times. He was patrolling."

I bit my tongue to stop the surge of insults about Gaian. "How have Finn and Cythera been overnight?"

"We're hungry," Finn said. "I had a couple of protein bars in my pockets, but they're long gone."

"Greetings, Finn," I said. "How's the head?"

"Getting better. I hunted around and found a couple of bottles of water in a drawer and some cereal bars, but there's nothing else to eat. I'll have to eat the books off the shelves if I get much hungrier."

"And Cythera?"

"She roused for about five minutes during the night. I got her to drink something, but she wasn't making any sense. She got hit hardest by whatever took us down."

"A flying candlestick attacked you," I said.

"And then some gross green fog," Zandra said. "Do you remember that?"

"Ouch. And yuck. Yeah, I do. No wonder my ears are ringing. How's Dimitri getting on with figuring out what's happening?"

"We've not seen him this morning," Zandra said. "We need a plan of action, though."

"He sounds like a decent guy. I just wish Cythera would wake so she can give him orders. Graduates fresh out of training never bend the rules."

"I expect you did. And I'm sure we can persuade him to bend if we need him to," I said. "We have our main suspects to tackle again today."

"What will you do?"

"We need to speak to Lila again. She keeps stressing that the beam accidentally fell. She even suggested lightning struck the building and damaged it."

"I suppose it's not impossible. The weather has been so odd recently."

"I was wondering if we should search her office. See if she's hiding any secrets."

"Be careful," Finn said. "If Lila's behind this and she figures out you're onto her, she's got power. If she can take me and Cythera out, you're not dealing with a lightweight magic user."

I nodded. "And we still have Mrs. Simister on the suspect list, but having spoken to her several times and again at dinner last night, I'm not sure she did it."

"We don't know her, though," Zandra said. "She could be lying about having had a happy marriage. Maybe they despised each other. She could have seen this as an opportunity to get rid of him and blame the crazy conditions in Crimson Cove. Or even pin the crime on somebody else."

"We could check through her things," I said. "But she didn't come in with luggage. We could go through her clothing."

Zandra shook her head. "She went to bed in her clothes. Remember, she said she was cold and couldn't get warm. She was shivering. That's why I got those extra blankets for her."

"What about Willow?" Finn said. "Any progress with the ghost?"

"She's nervous about something. Perhaps she's seen something that's worried her. She keeps saying it's all the people and the bad weather making her anxious, but until we know for sure how strong Willow is, we'll keep her on the list." I slid a glance at Sorcha. She was listening intently to the conversation, so I was unable to drop Gaian's name into the mix.

"Keep me up-to-date," Finn said. "And let me know when Dimitri is free to talk. We can compare notes, and I'll help him out if he needs it. Getting a difficult job like this with no experience will be making him sweat."

"It's time for breakfast. I'll go get Gaian." Sorcha stood from her seat. "We'll join you in a few minutes."

We headed off in separate directions. I went into the dining room to discover Vorana, Ember, Sage, and Dimitri were already there. He was no longer in a robe but wore his newly laundered clothes. Lila walked in, carrying a tray of delicious-smelling sausages and fried eggs.

She nodded a greeting when she saw us. "Right on time. How did you sleep?"

"Better now we have the couch." I hopped into a seat next to Zandra.

"I'm sorry about the sleeping arrangements." Lila set down the tray, and everyone helped themselves.

"You're doing an incredible job," Vorana said as she cut a sausage into small pieces for Sage. "None of us could have known this would happen. The room I'm in with Sorcha and Gaian is comfortable."

"It is." Gaian strolled in with Sorcha, looking refreshed after having a full night of sleep and not doing his share of looking after the angels. "Although I'll be glad to get out of here."

Everyone settled around the table and started on their food.

"I heard some strange sounds last night," Vorana said. "Scratching and scurrying noises."

"We've heard that too," Zandra said. "Coming from the attic?"

Vorana nodded. "It wasn't all the time, but it sounded as if something was moving around up there."

"It's probably rodents," Gaian said.

Lila dropped her knife. "No! The attic's been cleaned out and insulated."

"Rats can get in through any small spaces," Gaian said. "You only need to miss one tiny hole, and they'll be in and inviting their friends."

"I do not have rats. Don't tell people I have a problem with rodents when you get out of here, or I may as well not bother opening." Lila huffed out a breath.

"If we get out of here," I muttered. "It could be bats. They're a charming species, and they often roost in attics."

"They're protected," Gaian said. "If you've got bats, you've just been given a nice big bill to make sure they have all the creature comforts they desire."

"Bats I can handle. I've got no problem with them," Lila said. "But nothing is living in my attic."

"There's something up there," Vorana said. "I didn't imagine it. Sage heard it too."

Sage nodded but couldn't speak because her mouth was full of sausage.

"I didn't hear anything," Ember said. "My ears are better than Sage's. I'm sure I'd know if there were rats in this place. I'd be able to smell them."

"I'll look into it later," Lila said. "We have bigger concerns to deal with."

"I'll go take a look now." I jumped off my seat, not waiting for a response, and dashed out of the dining room and up the stairs. Then, instead of going into the attic, I doubled back down the stairs and into Lila's office. I'd only been in here briefly while we were looking for an escape route, so I hadn't paid much attention to what was in here.

The room was bland and impersonal. There was a mess of papers on the desk, a computer, and a desk chair. There was also a blanket and pillow next to the chair and a single cabinet with files. That was it. No pictures, no personal knickknacks on the desk, not even a favorite coffee mug. Maybe Lila had yet to move her things in, or she had her own place where she stayed when she wasn't working.

I walked around the side of the desk and discovered a briefcase. It was identical to the briefcase Doctor Simister had carried when he arrived at the inn. I glanced at the door to make sure no one was watching then pulled open the briefcase. There was a pile of folders inside. It was an odd item to bring on a day out with your wife. And if Doctor Simister was retired, why would he carry a briefcase full of folders with him?

I flipped through the papers, knowing I had little time before people started looking for me. Most of them were reports or billing statements. There was a file marked 'Crimson Cove.'

I was about to open it when footsteps approached the office, so I eased the briefcase shut and pushed it back into place. I held my breath as someone entered the office. I couldn't see who it was as they walked around the opposite side of the desk, but I edged around it so they didn't spot me snooping.

A drawer opened, so I took a risk and dashed out the door. I ran back upstairs and waited a moment before nonchalantly walking down. I returned to the dining room. Everyone was in their seats. So, who had been in the office?

"Any sign of rats?" Lila said when she saw me.

"You have no problems in your attic." I hopped back into my seat and gave Zandra a meaningful look.

"Really? Nothing? Are you sure you looked everywhere?" Gaian inspected a piece of toast then placed it on his plate.

"Of course. Pass me a sausage, Zandra."

"Where's Mrs. Simister?" Vorana asked. "I've not seen her this morning."

"I knocked on her door to let her know breakfast was ready," Lila said. "But there was no answer. I assumed she must be resting."

"Shock can exhaust a person," Vorana said. "We should save her something, though."

"She had a restless night," I said. "She was sleeping when we left the room."

"I'd like to speak to her," Dimitri said. "Perhaps someone could rouse her."

"I'll take her a breakfast tray." Lila stood from her chair. "I'll give her a strong cup of tea to get her moving." She hurried out of the dining room.

"What are you up to?" Zandra leaned over and whispered to me. "I know you didn't go into the attic."

"I'll tell you later," I said. "I found something interesting. Or should that be troubling?"

She arched an eyebrow but didn't press me further, since she knew some of the company we kept around the table couldn't be trusted.

I ignored Gaian as he waxed lyrical about his in-depth knowledge of plant-based alternatives for sausage and how they were so much better for you and helped myself to a large chunk of meatiness from Zandra's plate. I was contemplating whether I wanted a fried egg when there was a crash overhead, followed by a stomach-clenching scream.

"She's dead!"

Chapter 12

Frozen surprise

We stood around Mrs. Simister's bed. No one spoke. Everyone stared at her frozen corpse. Her eyes were open as she stared sightlessly at the ceiling, a film of frost covering all the visible parts of her body. But it wasn't the frost that interested me. It was the glowing white gremlin chaos symbols on her cheeks.

"How did this happen?" Lila was surrounded by the remains of the breakfast tray she'd brought up for Mrs. Simister. "We were all downstairs. Who did this?"

"Juno wasn't with us all the time." Gaian stood at the foot of the bed with Sorcha beside him.

I narrowed my eyes at him. "I have no motive for killing Mrs. Simister."

"You were the only one who wasn't in the dining room when this happened," he said.

"Untrue. While I was looking around... the attic, I heard footsteps. Somebody else left the dining room at the same time as me."

"I went to the kitchen for a moment," Lila said. "But I didn't have time to come up here and do this. I wouldn't even know how to cast such awful magic over someone."

"I went to the bathroom," Sorcha said. "But just like Lila, I was only gone for a few minutes."

Gaian rested his arm around her shoulders. "You wouldn't do something like this, babe. I vouch for you."

"Could she have been frozen before you left her this morning?" Gaian said to Zandra.

"I'd have noticed if we were sharing a room with a frosty corpse." Zandra tugged on the end of her hair. "Although she was bundled under a pile of blankets, so I didn't see her. And... and I didn't check on her. I was glad she'd stopped crying, and I didn't want to disturb her and set her off again."

"So, this could have happened anytime overnight," Lila said.

"I'd have heard if anyone came into our bedroom," I said. "My cat senses never let me down." I looked at Dimitri. He appeared almost as frozen as Mrs. Simister, staring at her body and not speaking. I nudged him with my head. "We should secure the scene."

He blinked several times then nodded. "Of course. Everyone needs to leave."

"Why bother?" Gaian said. "Any evidence won't be any good now. It's been contaminated since we've all been in here. And Lila made a mess when she dropped the tray."

"You'd have dropped it too." Lila's cheeks flushed. "I was shocked by what I found. When I pulled back the blanket, I didn't expect this!"

I hopped onto Zandra's shoulder as Dimitri gently ushered everyone out of the bedroom. "I didn't see Mrs. Simister this morning. Maybe this did happen last night."

"What about your cat senses not missing anything?" she whispered.

"I'm almost perfect, but even I have flaws. And I was tired. Someone could have translocated in here, cast the freeze spell over Mrs. Simister, and then left. It wouldn't have taken long. And if Mrs. Simister was asleep, she wouldn't have put up a fight."

"She was saying how cold she was last night," Zandra said. "Maybe it was a slow-acting spell. Someone could have used it on her yesterday."

"Which means anyone here could have done it."

Dimitri returned to the room. "You need to leave, too. I know you share this room with Mrs. Simister, so I'll take that into account with any evidence I find."

"We'll assist you in the search," I said. "It's what we'd do if Cythera and Finn were investigating. Cythera would insist on us being here. She highly values us."

Zandra smirked but remained silent.

Dimitri hesitated. "I'm not sure that's a good idea."

"We can tell you about the symbols on Mrs. Simister's face," I said. "Make use of our skills. We're all the backup you've got until Cythera and Finn get free."

He scratched absently at his chest. "I wondered what they were. Was it a ritualistic killing? I took a unit on ritualistic behavior at the Academy. That stuff gets dark."

"I don't know how Mrs. Simister is connected to the symbols, but they've been showing up around town," I said.

He kept scratching, only stopping when he saw me watching. "Sorry. Nervous habit. Someone mentioned there'd been graffiti appearing everywhere. It looks like this?"

"Not graffiti. Let me catch you up on the seriousness of this situation." I gave Dimitri a summary of my symbol discoveries and what I believed they meant.

"So, this lady has a connection to gremlins?" Dimitri didn't look convinced.

"Either that, or they targeted her for their own amusement," I said. "Gremlins enjoy casting a wide chaos net and then watching the fallout."

"What do these gremlins want with Crimson Cove?" Dimitri leaned over Mrs. Simister and studied the symbols. "And why kill two nice people and injure some angels? That's not chaos. That's cruel."

"They did it to keep us trapped and scared," Zandra said.

Dimitri stood and rubbed the back of his neck. "Maybe. I guess I'll have to find that out. But I'll be upfront with you two. I'm not sure where to start. Angel Force eases us in with simple cases to get us used to protocol. We're not let loose on murders for at least a year, and then we always have a mentor to advise and support us."

"You're up to the job," I said. "And Finn will answer any questions you may have. You should make use of his experience. And ours. We're really rather fabulous."

"We do okay," Zandra said. "We can unpick trouble when we have to. And this isn't our first dead body."

Dimitri's gaze flicked around the room. "Neither of you saw anything strange this morning before coming down to breakfast?"

"As far as we knew, Mrs. Simister was asleep," Zandra said. "She didn't stir when I used the bathroom, so we left her to it. She's been through a lot, so we figured she needed to rest."

"You didn't think it odd that, when you thumped around in the bathroom, it didn't wake her?"

"My witch doesn't thump," I said. "She can be very quiet. Besides, some people are sound sleepers."

Dimitri strode to the window and attempted to open it. "Still stuck. No one came in from outside."

"And we're not on a lower level, so they'd have needed to be inventive to get up here," I said. "But we'd have heard someone sliding the window open. No one came in that way."

"It was an inside job," Dimitri said. "The same person who killed her husband?"

Zandra shrugged. "Unless we've got two killers on our hands, but I'm really hoping we don't."

"Could Mrs. Simister have killed her husband, and this was a revenge killing?" Dimitri ran a hand through his hair.

"Whoever did it has a connection to the Simisters, yet everyone here claims they don't know them," I said.

Zandra arched an eyebrow. "Not everyone is telling the truth."

"I need a moment to think," Dimitri said. "It's a lot to process. And I don't have my manual to guide me."

"Be methodical," I said. "You can discount Finn and Cythera since they're injured and trapped inside a room. And, of course, we're innocent. And then—"

"Sorry to interrupt, but I don't know you," Dimitri said. "I have to consider you both suspects, especially since you were most likely the last to see Mrs. Simister alive."

I hissed out a gentle sigh. "You've heard from Finn how indispensable we are to Angel Force."

"I don't know Finn. I don't even know if the two people trapped in that room are actually angels."

"Of course they're angels," I said. "Why would we lie about that?"

Dimitri tugged at his bottom lip. "I can't take anything at face value. Until I see if that's Cythera and Finn behind the door, I must be cautious. They could be your accomplices, telling me anything I want to hear to ensure I don't suspect you."

"Give me strength," Zandra muttered under her breath.

"What if they show you their feathers?" I asked. "Finn won't mind losing a feather or two. He may be able to post one through the gap at the bottom of the door."

Dimitri considered this option. "Let's go speak to them."

"This is a waste of time," Zandra whispered to me as we headed down the stairs, leaving Mrs. Simister frozen in bed. "We should ditch this new recruit. He's slowing us down."

"I don't disagree, but we need to keep this angel on side, or we'll end up under house arrest because he thinks we're the killers."

We arrived at the guest sitting room. Vorana was taking a shift and sat in the seat by the locked door. Ember and Sage were nowhere to be seen. They were most likely finishing the breakfast leftovers. I never got around to having that delicious fried egg.

"Cythera's awake," she said. "I should warn you, she's grumpy. And she's mentioned a dress fitting several times. She seems more concerned about that than being trapped."

"She must have a concussion." Dimitri smoothed down the front of his shirt, smoothed his hair, then tapped on the door. "Hello? This is Dimitri from Angel Force."

"Who's that?" Cythera's tone was sharp.

"I'm a new recruit sent by Central Command. We've been trying to reach you to get an update on the magical upheaval in town."

"Finn told me about your arrival. I don't recognize your voice. Have we met?"

"No, but I know about you. It's an honor. Your reputation at the training academy is legendary."

"I'm sure it is," she muttered. "What's the situation out there?"

Dimitri cleared his throat. "I'm sorry to have to do this, but I need proof you're both angels."

"You need what?"

A red flush spread up Dimitri's neck. "It's just... I don't want to make a mistake. I can't see you, so I don't know you work at Angel Force."

"The guy's got a point," Finn said. "We could be anyone."

"Of course we're not anyone!" Cythera's sigh was so loud, we heard it on the other side of the door.

"Juno suggested you show me your feathers," Dimitri said.

"The cat's a genius. How do we do that? In case you aren't aware, we're trapped in this room. There's no food, barely any water left, and no bathroom."

"I set up a private wastebasket for us to use," Finn said. "It's not luxurious, but it does the job."

I held back a chuckle, but Zandra wasn't so discreet.

"I'm glad you find our imprisonment so entertaining, Miss Crypt," Cythera snarled.

"I see getting whacked on the head has only made her mood sourer," Zandra muttered to me. "I didn't know such a thing was possible."

"Perhaps you could put a feather under the door," I said. "I don't know how far it'll get before the magic repels it, but it would ease Dimitri's concerns that you're pretending to be someone you're not."

"We could try that," Finn said. "I've gotten my pinkie finger under there without it getting bitten off."

"There's enough space to do it. I was wondering if we could squeeze straws under the door so we could get them some more water," Vorana said.

"Which we'd have to lap off the floor like animals," Cythera grumbled.

"Let's stay positive," I said. "Once Dimitri knows who you are, we can press on with solving these murders and then getting you free. Wouldn't you like that?"

It took a few moments and several attempts, but finally, a white feather poked out from under the door. It didn't get far before it bent and exploded into ash.

"Happy now?" I said to Dimitri.

He nodded. "That looked like a genuine wing feather."

"It was. And it hurt to pull out," Finn said.

"I just needed to be careful. This is the strangest situation I've ever been in."

"Same here," I said. "But Cythera will extol our virtues. She's always happy to give us a glowing recommendation. Cythera, why don't you tell Dimitri how crucial we are to your work?"

Several seconds of silence passed.

"Zandra and her cat aren't terrible to work with. But watch that the cat doesn't overstep. She has a ridiculously high opinion of herself."

"You see! An endorsement I'd be thrilled to have on my tombstone. We're always happy to assist. And we don't even charge for our services." I tilted my head. "Perhaps we should. Cythera, how large is your budget for hiring consultants?"

I got a growl in response.

"Do they know about the second murder?" Dimitri whispered to Vorana.

She gave him an encouraging smile. "I filled them in."

He nodded. He kept nodding, his gaze flicking around as if seeking inspiration. Dimitri finally looked at me. "Um... so what do we do next?"

※※※※※

"Are you sure about this?" Dimitri tiptoed beside me as we headed to Lila's office.

"We need to know if she's keeping secrets. And we need to look inside Doctor Simister's briefcase. Zandra will keep Lila distracted. She won't know what we're doing." I guided Dimitri to Lila's office. I'd told him what I'd discovered when I'd been on my fake rat hunt, and he'd agreed Doctor Simister's briefcase in Lila's office needed looking into.

With Zandra in the kitchen, pretending to be interested in learning how to make a British sourdough scone with a brown sugar topping, we left her with Lila to go clue hunting.

"I'm sure there's an innocent explanation for why she has the briefcase," Dimitri whispered. "She may have been keeping it safe for Mrs. Simister."

"Or she stole it because it contains important information she doesn't want anyone else to discover."

"Like what?"

"That's what we're about to find out."

We reached Lila's office, and I checked no one was around then hurried inside with Dimitri and eased the door closed behind us.

The office was the same as the last time I'd visited. Papers were still scattered on the desk, and a blanket and pillow were on the floor beside the chair. I hurried around the side of the desk. The briefcase was gone.

"Where is it?" Dimitri asked.

"It's been moved. Whoever came in here when I was looking around must have realized they needed a better hiding place."

"Did you see anything that could help you identify who it was?" Dimitri looked through the papers on the desk.

"I didn't get a glimpse of them. I didn't dare risk it in case they caught me," I said. "They seemed to know where they were going. They went straight around the desk and opened a drawer. They must have hidden the briefcase after that."

"How does Lila know Doctor and Mrs. Simister?"

"She said she didn't know them. They weren't invited to the inn's preview event. They showed up at the last minute. Although she may not be telling the truth about their connection. Nobody knows much about Lila."

"I can't see anything here that causes me alarm about her," Dimitri said. "There's a lot of paperwork about the inn. Mainly bills and invoices. Perhaps you're making too much of this. Lila was being a responsible business owner and keeping a guest's briefcase safe. There was no malice behind her stashing it here."

I glanced over my shoulder at him as I examined a cobwebby corner. "Are you always this positive?"

"I like to see the good in people whenever I can."

"You may think differently after a few decades of working at Angel Force."

Dimitri appeared surprised by my comment but said nothing to contradict me.

"Don't you think it's odd a retired man carried a briefcase?" I asked.

"Not necessarily. It's a convenient way to carry things around."

"Do you have one?"

"Um... no. But I know a lot of people who do."

"When I looked inside it, it wasn't full of treats, leaflets to tourist attractions, or books. You know, the things you'd expect to take on a fun day out. And there was a file in there labeled Crimson Cove."

"What was in the file?"

"I didn't have time to see. I had to flee before I was caught," I said.

"Maybe the file was full of information about fun things to do here. Doctor Simister could have carried the briefcase most of his working life, so he got attached to it. People become sentimental about things like that."

"Sentimental enough to bring it on a day out with his wife? It doesn't make sense." By this time, I'd checked every nook and cranny of the office and found no sign of the briefcase.

"Perhaps these deaths aren't even connected," Dimitri said. "They happened in different ways. Crushing and freezing. If it's a serial killer—"

I hopped around and stared at him. "No one said anything about a serial killer!"

"I'm just making suggestions. They usually have a favored method of slaying. We did a unit on them at the Academy. Some like using dark spells. Others use corrosive potions. Some prefer a more hands-on approach. Strangulation. Knives. There was one extraordinary case involving a foot fetish. The killer would—"

"I know it's impolite to interrupt, but the deaths have one big thing in common," I said. "Both victims had gremlin chaos symbols on their bodies. That makes it likely the same person did it. Those symbols are old and have been out of use for a long time, so few people know about them."

"I need to learn more about these symbols," Dimitri said after a short pause. "And we should move Mrs. Simister. Perhaps settle her in with her late husband?"

I nodded my approval. At last, he was taking things seriously. "Follow me. We'll get Mrs. Simister comfy in the cellar, check the symbols on the corpses, then look at the floorboards, and I'll tell you all I know about the gremlins."

Chapter 13
Corpse comparison

Dimitri stood back from Doctor and Mrs. Simister's corpses. Several feet back, not looking keen on getting closer, even though he'd carried Mrs. Simister down the stairs into the cellar not five minutes ago. We'd been joined by Zandra and Sage, although Sage was almost asleep on her feet, barely able to keep her eyes open as she yawned, smacked her lips together, and shuffled about.

"Take a closer look at the bodies," I said to Dimitri. "They won't bite. Don't you want to study the symbols? They look almost identical."

"No, thank you. There's only so much corpse exposure I can handle in one day," Dimitri replied, his face the wrong shade of gone-off milk.

"The deaths must be connected, and these symbols connect them," I said.

Sage yawned loudly. "How are gremlins sneaking about this place without us seeing them?"

I had no answer to that question. The silence from the others showed they were just as stumped.

"It's not only in here that sneaky magic is a problem," Dimitri said. "If we don't get a handle on this, Crimson Cove will become a shadow of the place you remember."

"We're not letting that happen," Sage grumbled. "My witch loves this town."

"Almost as much as she loves me." Ember popped into view.

Sage hissed at him. "Stop doing that, you little creep. It's unsettling the way you appear out of nowhere, like some unwelcome furry fiend. Go away!"

"You're Vorana's familiar, is that right?" Dimitri asked Ember.

"No! Vorana is my witch. I'm the only familiar bonded to her. This fluffy jerk has made himself an unwelcome addition to the household. We don't want him." Sage growled at Ember.

"Sage, that's a terrible thing to say. I was openly invited into your home, and now you're not happy because Vorana prefers me to you." Ember strutted over to the bodies and sniffed them. "Have you figured out what happened? I'm happy to help if you're stuck. I can sneak in and out of places and listen in."

"So you can feed us lies," Sage said. "If you must be here, keep your opinions to yourself."

"If you don't want me, I can sit with Vorana. I'll tell her you were mean to me again. She won't want you anymore if you keep being so spiteful."

"Stop antagonizing each other," I said. "Put your personal issues to one side and focus on the murders. If we don't figure out what's going on soon, none of us will have any homes to return to."

Ember sniffed. "It's all Sage's fault we argue."

I stomped over to the feisty kitten and boxed his ears. "Untrue. You're provoking her. Sage thought she was doing a good thing by inviting you into the family, but you've exploited her kind nature. Vorana and Sage are wonderful together. Stop messing with that relationship, or you'll regret it."

"Did you hear that?" Ember's wide eyes turned to Dimitri. "I just got threatened. That's a crime, isn't it?"

Dimitri's forehead wrinkled, and confusion crossed his face. "I'm not sure what's going on here."

"Rest assured, it has nothing to do with this investigation. Ember and Sage have issues to iron out. They'll do it on their own time when we have less pressing things to sort out. Got it?" I bared my teeth at Ember then glared at Sage.

Ember huffed out several disgruntled breaths but then sat on the floor and curled his tail around his paws. "I'm not a troublemaker."

"Neither am I," Sage said.

There was a moment of tense, awkward silence as we stared at the bodies. Dimitri, once again, seemed stuck as to what to do next, so I helped him out.

"Let's cover them both and go look at the floorboard in the guest bedroom," I said. "You'll see the similarities between the symbols. That should help you make a plan of attack."

"Yes! Excellent idea." Dimitri was the first up the stairs, although everyone was grateful to leave the corpse-scented cellar and head up to the brighter rooms.

I made sure Lila wasn't around to see what we were up to and hurried everyone into the guest bedroom. I revealed the symbols to Dimitri, and he took a moment to inspect them, crouched by the floorboard, one hand resting under his chin.

"Since Lila owns this inn, she could have put these here," he said. "That must make her our prime suspect."

"Or the symbols were here before she moved in," I said.

"Or someone put them there during the renovation," Zandra said. "Lila had dozens of different trades coming in and out. It wouldn't have been hard for someone to wander in pretending they worked here and leave them."

"I think it was Willow," Ember said. "She's sneaky and flits in and out of places. She always leaves behind a cold draft."

"You're as sneaky as that ghost," Sage said.

"I've always been honest with you," Ember said. "You just don't like hearing the truth."

"You have a funny idea of what the truth is."

"Let's focus on the murders," I said. "Ember, have you seen anything that makes you suspicious of Willow?"

He nodded, his angry glare drifting from Sage. "I saw her going into Mrs. Simister's room late last night."

"She was in our room?" Zandra said. "When was this?"

"I got up to stretch and check everyone was safe, like a good familiar. I was quiet, so I didn't disturb anyone, and as I was tiptoeing back to our room, I saw her. It must have been about four in the morning."

"What did she do?" I asked.

"Willow was anxious. She swirled back and forth along the wall for several seconds before disappearing through it. You didn't sense her?"

"No. But we were asleep," Zandra said.

"She could have just been looking around, checking in on us," I said. "I'd have felt the presence of a ghost in the bedroom. And Willow usually announces her arrival with a drop in temperature and flickering lights."

"We were tired," Zandra said. "Maybe we didn't wake when she showed up."

"Does Willow know Doctor and Mrs. Simister?" Dimitri asked.

I shook my head. "She's been here for hundreds of years, and their paths have never crossed."

"She could be lying," Ember said.

"You'd know about that since you're the expert in lying," Sage said.

"I'm telling the truth!" Ember's hackles rose. "And I'm certain it wasn't Vorana. Or do you want to make her a suspect and ignore that sneaky, troubled ghost?"

"Of course I don't, you dumb fuzzy jerk. Vorana would never do anything like this. My witch is innocent." Sage's hackles also lifted as the tension ricocheted up.

"*Our* witch is innocent," Ember said. "And so are Gaian and Sorcha. They were asleep in the room when I left."

I looked at Sage. "Did you hear anyone get up and leave your room that night?"

She wrinkled her nose. "I suppose someone could have left, but it wasn't Vorana. I was curled up by her head all night. I was whacked out and slept straight through."

"So, the inn's resident ghost is guilty of these crimes?" Dimitri said. "Does she have the power to pull down ceiling beams and freeze a person to death?"

"It's something we've been discussing," I said. "Willow must have some power since she's survived in her original form for so long. Ancient ghosts often get wispy and misshapen."

"I saw Willow watching Doctor and Mrs. Simister," Ember said. "I didn't like the look in her eyes. It gave me the shivers."

"When was that?" Sage said. "Willow wasn't around much on the first night."

"That you saw! Your eyesight is going, so you always miss things. Willow was there, sticking to the shadows and watching us. And she paid particular attention to the unexpected arrivals. I'm certain she knew them."

"We need to find this ghost," Dimitri said. "The more I'm hearing about her, the more concerned I'm becoming."

"We may find her near the attic," I said. "She's concerned about the rodents up there."

Dimitri shuddered. "Rats are almost as bad as corpses. Come on. Let's go find this ghost."

We left the guest bedroom, and it only took us a moment to discover Willow drifting along the corridor, close to the attic stairs.

"Be careful of her," Ember whispered. "She's dangerous."

"Quiet," Sage hissed at him. "You don't know what you're talking about."

"I'll show you. I'll catch the killer, and Vorana will be proud of me. She'll make me her full-time familiar and put you in a retirement home for worn-out, unwanted creatures that nobody likes."

I boxed his ears again. "Sage is a magnificent familiar, and she'll never be replaced."

"So you reckon," Ember muttered under his breath.

The more time I spent with this young cat, the more I realized I didn't know him. When we first met, his demeanor had been sweet, but had that been an act to worm his way into our lives? Was this unpleasant, harshly spoken creature the true Ember?

Ember bounded ahead of the group, his tail up. "What were you doing in Mrs. Simister's room last night?"

"I'll ask the questions." Dimitri's wings fluttered as he hurried to join Ember. "I'm Dimitri. I'm investigating the two recent deaths."

Willow stopped moving and was staring down at Ember. "What about them?"

Dimitri patted his chest to get her attention. "Could you tell me if you had a connection to the victims?"

She shook her head, lifting her gaze to study him. "No. I didn't know them."

"You did," Ember said. "I saw you watching them. And you weren't happy they were here."

Willow's eyebrows lowered. "I'd never met them before. Why would I watch two strangers?"

"Because you're keeping secrets," Ember said. "Tell us the truth. Why did you kill the Simisters?"

"Ember! Let's not get ahead of ourselves." Dimitri tried to pick him up, but Ember hissed and scratched Dimitri's hand.

He backed away from the spunky young cat, clutching his injured hand. "Willow, could you tell me your movements last night?"

"Why? What do you think I've done?" Willow's form flickered along with the corridor lights.

"We have a witness who saw you go into Mrs. Simister's bedroom in the early hours of the morning."

"An unreliable witness," Sage muttered.

Willow's terrified gaze flicked around the group. She visibly shrank. "I went in her room. But I went into all the rooms. I like making sure everyone is safe. I may not be able to help, but I can alert others if there's any trouble. This place has felt unstable since the work was completed. It's a different space. I'm not sure I like it."

"What do you mean?" I asked. "You sense different magic?"

Willow nodded. "Something's changed. I sense the vibrations of unhappy magic. It's been quiet here for such a long time, and then there was this explosion of power. I can't figure out where it came from."

"Maybe the renovation work stirred something up," Zandra said. "That can happen when old buildings are repaired. The walls absorb some of the past. Especially if that past is troubled."

"I don't know about that, but I believed Mrs. Simister when she said there was a darkness in this place."

"You have been snooping in on her conversations!" Ember said. "I knew it."

"No! I mean, not specifically her conversations. I wanted to know what was going on, and I agreed to help Juno. I'm scared this place is unsafe, and I'm trapped."

"Stop telling lies." Ember shot out an orange-tinged spell that flew over Willow's head and hit the wall.

Sage hissed and swiped her paw at Ember, who dodged just in time. Sage spat, her scruffy fur bristling with anger. Her harness jingled as she hobbled closer to him.

Ember flicked his tail and smirked. "I'm not afraid of you, old-timer." He jabbed at Sage's ear, his claws out. "I'm faster and stronger than you."

"Stop that!" I ordered.

Sage yowled and hurled a spell at him. A fierce wind knocked Ember off his paws, but he regained his balance and countered with a blast of fire. The flames singed Sage's fur, and she hissed in pain.

"You're reckless and inexperienced," Sage snarled, spitting a glowing green ball at him. Ember leapt out of the way, and the ball hit the wall, creating an explosion of jagged sparkles.

"I'm not the one who needs a harness to walk," Ember taunted, his black and white fur fluffed in excitement.

Sage's eyes narrowed. "Age and experience matter more than looks and supple joints." She growled, sending another spell his way.

Ember batted it aside with a paw. He leaped at her with claws bared.

Sage dodged and weaved, trying to land a hit. They tumbled and rolled across the floor, knocking over ornament tables, until Sage pinned Ember with a paw.

"Stay away from my witch," she hissed, her eyes glowing with magic.

Ember glared up at her, his own eyes blazing with defiance. A bolt of lightning appeared as he whipped his tail from side to side.

The bolt hit Sage's paw, and she yelped in pain. She staggered back, releasing Ember from her grasp. The two cats glared at each other, panting and hissing.

I'd had enough. I leapt on Ember's back to stop him from throwing the next blast of magic. He twisted around, kicked me in the stomach, and thumped me with the spell intended for Sage. His power bounced through my body, leaving behind a painful sting. This kitten's magic hurt. He twirled and hit Willow with another wallop of magic. He followed it up with a glittering ball of power that surrounded the ghost and made her groan.

By the time I'd rolled onto my paws, Willow's form had dwindled to a wisp, and she held out a hand in submission. "Stop. I'm almost drained of energy. So much negativity."

It surprised me she'd given up so fast. She couldn't be that powerful if she faded after a couple of magic hits, but her form was barely visible as she swirled on the air currents.

"That kitten is lying. It wasn't me," she whispered.

"I told you Ember can't be trusted." Sage sniffed at her singed fur. "Look what he just did. He's out of control."

"I can! I saw Willow. Why would I lie? I want my witch safe and out of here, and I'll do anything to make sure that happens." Ember glowered at Willow.

"She's my witch!" Sage flung herself on Ember. They rolled around on the floor, hissing and snarling as fur flew and claws slashed through the air.

Even though I was still recovering from Ember's nasty spell, I dived between them and yanked Ember back by his scruff.

"This wasn't how you were trained to behave at the Academy. Show some restraint."

Ember's hackles were raised, and he hissed at me and clawed the air.

I looked at Dimitri. "Do something! You're supposed to be in charge."

"Um... Sure. Why don't we take a break and get something to eat?"

Chapter 14

Shocking hunt

We were sitting around the dining table again with everyone. Sage sat on one side of Vorana and Ember the other, both of them shooting spiteful glares at each other whenever they could. At least the fighting had stopped.

The wind screamed outside, banging invisible fists against the glass. Lila had made sandwiches for us, and there was a fruit platter for dessert.

I glanced at Dimitri several times, waiting to see what brilliant ideas he had for figuring out what to do next.

"Good sandwiches," he said with his mouth full. "Cheese is my favorite. What kind is it?"

"It's just cheddar," Lila said. "I didn't expect to have guests stay yet, so the longer we're here, the more basic the food will become."

"I could live off cheese sandwiches." Dimitri stuffed another one into his mouth and chewed.

I exchanged a glance with Zandra. Was he only going to talk about his sandwich and not get to the serious business of murder and the possibility our resident ghost was behind the killings?

"Do you grow those apples in the yard?" Dimitri pointed at the fruit platter. "This place comes with land, doesn't it?"

"I was thinking of planting apple trees, but that's way down on my list of priorities." Lila sipped from her mug of tea. "And the way things are going, I may not even get to open."

"Once Angel Force has this investigation fully underway, things will soon resolve. Right, Dimitri?" I said.

He finished his sandwich and brushed crumbs off his fingers. "Of course."

"And...?" I prompted.

"And what?"

"What should we do next? We have two bodies, suspects, but nothing in the way of a motive. Mrs. Simister didn't freeze to death by accident. Somebody did that to her. And it seems likely someone damaged the beam so it would squash her husband. And then we have the matching symbols the victims have on them."

Dimitri reached for another sandwich. I resisted the urge to slap him with a murder mitten and tell him to get a move on. He checked what was inside the sandwich and then nodded.

"Perhaps we should go over everyone's movements from last night?" I spoke through gritted teeth.

"Good idea. Check alibis," Dimitri said. "Who wants to go first?"

I held in a sigh. This rookie had a lot to learn.

"I was in my office all night," Lila said. "Once we had dinner, I tidied the kitchen, did some paperwork, and then went to sleep."

I waited for Dimitri to ask follow-up questions. He just ate his sandwich.

"You stayed there all night?" I asked.

She nodded. "It didn't feel safe to walk around alone, not with everything that's happening. I even wedged a chair against the door so no one could get in while I was sleeping."

"So, you were alone all night?" I said, giving Dimitri a pointed look.

"Yes. But I had nothing to do with what happened to Mrs. Simister," Lila said.

I'd yet to figure out if Lila had any connection with Doctor and Mrs. Simister, but I couldn't see a motive for wanting them dead. Although she had kept Doctor Simister's briefcase. Were the contents of the briefcase worth killing over?

"We were in the guest bedroom," Gaian said, gesturing to Sorcha. "Along with Vorana."

Vorana nodded. "We all went to bed around the same time. Sage and Ember stayed with me. We're on the cot bed. It's meant for children, but we can just about fit. Sage slept by my head like she usually does, and Ember was by my feet."

"Ember, you left the bedroom, didn't you?" I said.

His nose twitched. "I didn't hide that from you. I'm glad I left, though, because I saw the killer in action."

"Let's not make assumptions," I said. "You saw Willow floating around, but did you see her do anything to Mrs. Simister?"

"Well, no. But it was suspicious behavior. And we all saw how anxious she became when we confronted her."

"Willow was anxious because we questioned her about being a murderer," I said. "And there was an overly enthusiastic cat throwing spells around and hurting her."

"It sounds like you were harsh on that ghost," Vorana said. "You should have given Willow a chance to explain what she was doing."

"I was protecting you!" Ember said. "I had to make sure she couldn't hurt you. That's my job."

Sage grumbled to herself.

"I've never once felt uncomfortable around Willow," Vorana said. "She seems like a sweet ghost. We should give her a chance to explain why she went into Mrs. Simister's bedroom."

"If she came in, we didn't see her," I said. "We were there the whole night too. Nothing disturbed us."

"You must be losing your edge," Gaian said. "Unless one of you two did it."

"We're innocent of all crimes." I refused to be riled by Gaian's blunt foolishness. "Neither I nor my wonderful witch would hurt an innocent old woman."

"How do we know you didn't know her?" Gaian asked. "You could be hiding things from us."

"We can trust Zandra and Juno," Sorcha said quietly. "They always look out for other people."

Gaian's smug smile faded. "I've told you before, you're too trusting. It'll get you in trouble."

"Which is apparent because she's associating with him," I whispered to Zandra.

Zandra smirked and lifted her eyebrows.

"We're not involved in either of these deaths," I said. "And we can also rule out Finn and Cythera, since they're still trapped and injured."

"I was alone most of the night too," Dimitri said. "I patrolled the building to make sure nothing unpleasant happened."

"Like an old lady getting frozen to death in her bed?" I said.

He blushed. "I took a few breaks, and I may have dozed off a couple of times. That must have been when the killer struck."

"I saw Dimitri walking around," Sorcha said. "He came to check on me and the angels several times. He was doing his best. It's hard to stay awake all night when you have nothing to keep you occupied."

"It's not Dimitri's fault the killer struck again," Ember said. "It's that sneaky ghost. It's only because I have excellent eyesight that I spotted her snooping outside your bedroom. Maybe she had designs to kill you and Zandra as well, but something interrupted her. It could have been me or Dimitri patrolling."

With everyone in the room, it was hard to point fingers at the suspects on my list. Since Lila had been alone all night, it was possible she snuck out of her office, crept into the bedroom, and dealt the freezing death blow. And I still had my suspicions about Gaian, although it would have been hard for him to leave without being noticed since he was sharing with Sorcha, Vorana, Sage, and Ember.

"I'm championing Willow as the killer," Ember said. "And she's not here, which is doubly suspicious."

"She's not here because you injured her," Sage said. "Your attack was unnecessarily vicious."

"Someone had to take action. I don't trust her."

"What motive does she have for wanting Doctor or Mrs. Simister dead?" I asked.

"Maybe they argued. Or... or Willow scared Mrs. Simister, and she accidentally injured her with a spell. I don't know! But I know she's deceitful."

"Takes one to know one," Sage muttered.

Ember fired a hiss at Sage.

"You don't know Willow," I said to Ember.

"Neither do you! Why are you so willing to support a strange ghost, anyway? Have you and your witch got something to hide? Are you working with Willow?" Ember's fur bristled.

I growled at the impertinent kitten. "We always seek justice. We work with the angels, not against them."

"That's what I'm doing by showing you the evidence. It has to be Willow."

"I like the idea that Willow's guilty," Gaian said. "Dimitri, what do you think?"

Dimitri almost dropped the sandwich he was munching on. "I think we don't have much evidence, and we shouldn't jump to conclusions about what's going on."

I nodded my approval.

"You must have gotten the lay of the land by now. You're a trained expert from Angel Force. I'm interested in your opinion. What do your instincts tell you? Was it Willow?" Gaian leaned forward and rested his elbows on the table.

"I... I don't want to make assumptions." Dimitri took several seconds to set down his sandwich and rearrange himself in the chair. "It's hard to do proper research and form an opinion without additional resources."

"What additional resources do you need?" Gaian said. "We're here to help. You've got your training to back you up, and you have your angel instincts."

"Dimitri's already told you that he doesn't want to jump to conclusions and apprehend the wrong person," I said.

Gaian ignored me. "Who looks like the obvious killer? Is it anyone in here? Do you think any of us are untrustworthy?"

"I couldn't say." Dimitri shifted in his seat. "I should speak to Cythera. See what her opinion is of this situation."

"You don't want to get her involved. Cythera is unhappy, injured, and hungry. She won't make a rational decision while she's in that state. She may get overly emotional, too. My dealings with Cythera show she makes poorly considered decisions when her back is against the wall."

"I've had my run-ins with Cythera, but she gets things right in the end," I said.

"Why bother her?" Gaian said. "Or are you too afraid to step up and make a decision, Dimitri? Perhaps you haven't been truthful about your training. Were you bottom of the class? Failed key units? Or aren't you capable enough to be put in charge of a case like this?"

"I excelled in my classes!" Dimitri tugged at his shirt collar. "I was in the top twenty percent in some of them."

"Was there anything you struggled with, though? I can tell you're not a full angel, and I know some mixtures of magical beings find it hard to follow angel teachings. The angels have a particular template for learning." Gaian raised his hands. "I'm not saying this to be unkind, but if you're struggling, then we're here to support you. We must get this right."

Dimitri gulped. "Maybe there were units I didn't do so well in. But I graduated! The angels wouldn't have let me join a team if they didn't think I was capable."

"Or they knew your limits," Gaian said. "They were willing to employ you, but not to investigate anything as serious as a double murder. Just say the word, and we'll take the strain off. It can't be a fun position to be in, stepping into this chaos and not knowing which way to turn."

"Gaian is bullying him," I whispered to Zandra.

Zandra frowned. "You're pushing Dimitri before he's ready to make a decision."

"I'm offering help," Gaian said. "He's got information overwhelm. I'm letting him see which way he needs to go."

"Which way is that?" Dimitri asked. "What should I do?"

"Not listen to Gaian or be influenced by him," I said.

"Have I put your nose out of joint, Juno?" Gaian leaned back in his seat. "You always want to be the one to solve the puzzle."

I bristled at his insolence. "Why are you so keen on pointing the finger at Willow?"

"I'm following the evidence. We've gone through where everyone was, and Ember saw Willow outside Mrs. Simister's bedroom. If I were you, Dimitri, I'd start there. Tackle that ghost," Gaian said.

"What's Willow's motive for murder?" My hackles lifted as Gaian's expression grew smug.

"For all we know, it could be an old family feud that reared its head." Gaian shrugged. "You'll have to ask her."

"So, Willow's held a grudge for hundreds of years and rained down fury on two strangers who share a surname with someone from her ancestor's past?" I snorted my disbelief.

"There's no need to attack me. I'm simply making suggestions to be helpful," Gaian said. "We need to get the truth from Willow as soon as possible. The sooner we can find her and get answers, the safer we'll be."

"Do you think Willow wants to hurt all of us?" Lila said.

"Why stop at Doctor and Mrs. Simister? We're all still trapped. The magic keeping us here hasn't dropped now they're dead."

"Willow wants to pick us off one by one?" Dimitri's face paled.

I glared at Gaian. "Of course she doesn't. We must stop fear mongering and jumping to conclusions. Why would a seemingly benevolent ghost who's been here for hundreds of years turn into a rabid killer?"

"Have you seen outside?" Gaian said. "Crimson Cove is in chaos. That chaos could be affecting all of us."

"Gaian has a point. I've been getting terrible mood swings," Vorana said. "I yelled at everyone. Although, I stopped feeling like that when we got here. My bad mood lifted. Could the weird magic influence people in different ways?"

"Maybe it does," Gaian said. "Willow used to be a decent ghost, but something has warped her."

"Like what?" Was Gaian alluding to his knowledge of the gremlin chaos symbols?

He shrugged again. "I couldn't tell you, but this place is messed up and out of control. Maybe Willow's behind it all. Or she could be working with other entities to destabilize the town."

"She's gone from killer to destroyer of towns?"

"I'm looking for answers, just like you." Gaian stared at Dimitri. "Ghosts can be vicious if they're not cared for. Don't you agree?"

This made no sense. Why was Gaian going after Willow so hard? Did he realize people were looking at him and asking questions, and he needed a scapegoat?

"Dimitri, we're running out of time," Gaian said. "We must find Willow. She needs to be destroyed."

"Whoa! When did we start talking about destroying Willow?" I jumped onto the table.

"That's harsh and unnecessary," Vorana said. "Let's find her and just ask her a few questions."

"The time for questioning is gone," Gaian said. "If we don't deal with this ghost now, we could all be dead. I don't want to go to sleep again knowing she's roaming the corridors, figuring out how to enact her next murder."

"I don't have the authority to destroy a ghost." Dimitri stumbled over his words.

"Until we destroy her, we won't get free," Gaian said. "If she's the power base keeping us trapped, we need to neutralize her."

"No one is killing that ghost." I thumped my paws on the table.

"Why are you so worried about what happens to Willow?" Gaian said. "I hear you're always up for some obliteration when someone you don't like gets in your way."

I hissed at him, and he smirked back.

"Dimitri, I suggest you organize a search party," Gaian said, pushing back his seat and standing. "We need to start this ghost hunt before it's too late."

Chapter 15

Hunting party

It had only taken a few more minutes of persuasion from Gaian before Dimitri was on board with hunting Willow. Fortunately, he hadn't been convinced to destroy the ghost, but I was concerned it would only be a matter of time.

Dimitri, Gaian, and Sorcha had left the room to make preparations to hunt Willow. That left me with Vorana, Ember, Sage, and Lila.

"Have you ever had concerns about Willow?" I asked Lila as she cleared the table.

She hurriedly stacked plates. "Generally, she's been fine. She keeps out of everyone's way most of the time."

"Willow told us you were nice to her," Zandra said. "You made time to stop for a chat in the afternoons."

"Now and again. I got the impression Willow was lonely. She doesn't have great social skills, so I took pity on her."

"Has she ever done anything to scare you?" Vorana said.

Lila hesitated, a pile of plates in her hands. "Occasionally, some of the things she says worry me. I don't think she had a good life, and obviously, being trapped by a hex warps the mind. Her topics of conversation could get dark. I think she lost a lot of people to illness and poverty when she was alive."

"You think she's troubled?" Zandra said. "I didn't get that impression the few times we've seen her."

"I don't know about troubled, but how can anyone stay sane given her situation?" Lila bit her bottom lip. "She could be creepy. I hoped I could factor in the haunted inn angle as a tourist attraction. Willow would be this fun, adorable ghost that danced around and made people laugh with silly scares. But if guests meet her when she's in one of her dark moods and talking about the Black Death or the uncle who took two days to die from hanging, that wouldn't get me a five-star rating."

"You support what Gaian wants to do to her?" I asked.

"I'm not sure. I'll think about it while I'm clearing the kitchen," Lila said. "Maybe getting rid of Willow is for the best. My inn will no longer be haunted, and if she is behind what's happening, once she's gone, her power will vanish too. We can get out."

I hopped onto Zandra's lap as Lila left the room. "I don't like this. This ghost hunt could end in tragedy."

"I'm helping them," Ember said. "It's the right thing to do. Vorana, you stay here. I don't want you getting injured if the ghost turns nasty."

"I'm absolutely getting involved," Vorana said. "And I support Juno. We shouldn't destroy Willow because we have a few suspicions about her."

"She's hiding from us!" Ember said. "She should be here, defending herself."

"Willow is hiding because she's recovering after your fight," I said. "A fight you started. You gravely injured that ghost, so it'll take her time to recover."

"I'll never apologize for defending my witch. I had to neutralize Willow before she came after Vorana."

"It's sweet that you always look after me." Vorana petted Ember's head. "But I've never felt under threat by Willow. And I know how to look after myself."

"And she has me. Her actual familiar," Sage said. "I'll always be there if Vorana is in danger."

Vorana gently straightened Sage's harness. "I know you will. You both take care of me. But we can't let this happen to Willow. It's wrong to let fear take over and make us lose our senses."

"Who's joining us?" Gaian appeared in the doorway. He held two small roughhewn pots. "I've charged these with magic. They'll work as restraining jars until we figure out how to destroy Willow."

"We're coming with you." Zandra lifted me onto her shoulder as she stood.

"So are we," Vorana said.

I knew my witch, and there was no way she'd support Gaian in his deceitful scheme to destroy Willow. We were going to make sure he didn't misbehave.

"Which one of you can I trust with this?" Gaian held out a pot.

"I'll take it," Vorana said. "When I first opened the bookstore, I had a troublesome ghost as a resident. I thought we'd be able to get along, but he kept damaging the stock. In the end, I had to trap him. I sent him somewhere nice, though. He's haunting a wood five-hundred miles from here."

"It sounds like you can handle your ghosts. Good. At least I can rely on you." Gaian's gaze flicked to us. "Don't mess this up. I'm doing this for all of us. Banish this ghost, and we get free."

"If we trust your assumptions, we do," I said.

"I'm never wrong. Follow me. We're doing a room-by-room search."

"Where's Dimitri?" We followed Gaian out of the dining room and to the bottom of the main staircase.

"He's checking in with the other angels. I told him not to waste his time, since they're trapped, but he didn't listen." Gaian pointed toward the cellar door. "We'll start in the cellar and work our way up. That way, Willow can't escape."

"We'll join you in a few minutes," I said. "I need to speak to Finn."

"Suit yourself." He strode off to the cellar steps, where the others were waiting for him.

"What's the plan?" Zandra whispered.

"Let's see what the angels are discussing," I said. "We need to make sure Dimitri doesn't put any dumb ideas into Cythera's head about Willow being guilty."

Zandra hurried along the corridor to the guest sitting room. Dimitri stood outside the door, his head bent as he listened to Cythera.

"Of course, I understand," he said.

"What does Cythera think of the plan to catch Willow?" I asked.

Dimitri straightened. "I've told her about our concerns."

"You mean Gaian's concerns," I said. "I'm not convinced Willow is behind these murders."

"What makes you say that?" Cythera said from the other side of the door.

"Lack of motive, for one. And an unreliable witness."

"You don't think Ember can be relied upon?" Dimitri said.

"I know a few things about that young cat. He's not been honest in certain areas of his life, including how he joined Vorana's household. His personality has also changed since I met him," I replied.

"He's a young cat growing into his skills," Dimitri said. "You shouldn't hold that against him."

"You should trust Juno's instincts," Finn said. "She's often right about these things."

"Ember was convincing when he laid out his argument about Willow being the killer." Dimitri scrubbed at his forehead. "I need more support to figure this out. I don't want to do the wrong thing."

"You'll do a good job," Cythera said. "Take it slowly and review all the evidence."

"I was wondering about deputizing Gaian. He's knowledgeable and level-headed."

I couldn't stop the note of disgust slipping out of my mouth. "That's the worst idea I've ever heard. Gaian is a troublemaker. He stirred up the group so they'd go on this insane ghost hunt. He wants to destroy Willow before she can clear her name."

"Willow won't be destroyed," Cythera said. "I won't allow it."

"No offense, but you're trapped and injured. You're no use to us."

There was silence for a second, and I could imagine Cythera was scowling.

"It was just an idea," Dimitri said. "But I need a sounding board. This is overwhelming."

"Make use of Juno and Zandra," Finn said. "They've helped me out of plenty of tricky situations."

"But... I don't know them."

"And you know Gaian?" I said. "You're only interested in his support because he was the one who shouted loudest and bullied you into this hunt."

"He had useful ideas about how we can catch the killer and get out of here." Dimitri's cheeks flushed a dull red.

"Gaian twisted your arm when we were in the dining room," Zandra said. "He forced you into making a decision by suggesting you didn't know what you were doing. Tell him you've changed your mind about hunting Willow, and you want to interview each of us to see if there are holes in our stories. That'll buy us some time."

"It's what Cythera's finest angels would do," I said. "Don't let Gaian railroad you."

"And don't let that cat and Zandra do the same," Cythera said.

"Hey! We're on your side. We're fighting to stop an injustice from taking place," I said.

There was more silence from the locked room.

"I see no harm in talking to Willow first," Dimitri said. "As Ember pointed out, it is strange she's not around to defend herself."

"Would you hang out with this group when one of its members injured you?" I asked. "Willow is hiding and licking her wounds. She's giving herself time to regenerate."

"So she can attack us again." Dimitri shook his head. "I can't allow that. It's irresponsible."

"Has anyone seen Willow since she was injured?" Finn said.

"After the fight, she faded away," I said. "I haven't seen her since then."

"I wondered if it was her making this room so cold. It's been getting worse these past few hours. Some spell is messing with us in here," Finn said.

"It must be Willow. No one else could break through the magic." Dimitri pulled back his shoulders. "I won't let her harm you."

"Finn, can you see Willow in the room with you?" I said.

"No, but if she's injured, she may only be a faint mist," Finn replied. "I've looked around, but it would be easy for her to hide. But it's colder than a polar bear's Christmas in here."

"You see! We must find this ghost so we can get answers," Dimitri said.

"We may have some answers for you," Finn said. "Since we've been stuck in here, we've been going through the books on the shelves. Lila has quite a collection, and a lot of it is on the local history of Crimson Cove, including this inn."

"You found out something useful?" I asked.

"We found out about Willow," Finn said. "There's a book about when the inn was built, who owned it, and some of the people who lived and worked here. Willow was among them. Her full name is Willow Merlin."

"What power did she have when she was alive?" Zandra said.

"This is where it gets interesting. She was an elemental witch. She could control fire, air, water, and earth."

"Which means she was much more powerful than she let on when we questioned her." A shiver of concern twitched down my spine. "Why would someone with so much magic take on a servant's role? And why would she allow herself to get hexed by the owner?"

"We don't have those details," Finn said. "But it would be easy for her to alter temperatures and even mess with the weather."

"You think this ghost is behind everything that's going on in Crimson Cove?" Dimitri's expression grew concerned. "That makes it even more important we find her."

"I wouldn't go that far," Finn said. "But maybe she's not working alone. Although, someone with that kind of power could easily crack wood. Willow could have damaged the beam that killed Doctor Simister."

"Do you think she's coming for you?" Dimitri said. "Is that why the room is getting so cold?"

"I can't say for certain," Finn said. "But it is uncomfortable in here. I'll have to snuggle with Cythera if it gets worse."

"Don't be ridiculous," Cythera snapped. "Although we don't have all the information about the suspects, I agree with Gaian and Dimitri. You need to track down Willow. She's been hiding how powerful she is, and now the net is closing in, she's becoming desperate. A desperate criminal is a dangerous one, especially when they have that level of ability."

"But in her ghost form, she won't be so powerful," I said.

"Whatever she is, she's not safe to be around," Dimitri said. "We should join the others and hunt her down."

"We've got her!" Gaian's voice echoed down the main staircase.

I looked at Zandra, and she took off running, holding me tight on her shoulder so I didn't fall.

If Willow had been caught, we had to get to her before Gaian destroyed her and took away the only source of answers to the questions we'd just uncovered.

Chapter 16

Killer caught?

Willow cowered in the corner of an unfurnished guest bedroom. The lights flickered overhead as Gaian loomed over her with the restraining pot held out. Sorcha stood beside him with Lila on the other side, looking nervous. Vorana stood by the door with Sage and Ember.

"Hurry!" Vorana said when she saw us. "They've cornered her. Gaian threw some sort of spell at Willow so she can't move. He threatened to destroy her if she didn't confess."

Gaian glanced over his shoulder. "It's no less than she deserves. Two people are dead, angels are injured, and we've been held prisoner."

"Not necessarily by Willow." I hopped off Zandra's shoulder and stepped into the room. "We must give her a chance to talk, so she can tell us what she knows."

"There's no time left to talk." Gaian held the pot in one hand as he thrust out his other palm. A blast of green magic slammed into Willow.

She groaned and curled into a ball, crouching even lower in the corner.

"Maybe you shouldn't do that," Sorcha whispered. "We should let Willow speak. It's only fair."

"Fair! How is the way she's treated us fair? She's trapped us, scared us, and put your life at risk. That's unacceptable."

"I agree, but we need to be certain she's behind this." Sorcha touched Gaian's arm, but he shook her fingers off him.

"It must be her," he snapped. "Dimitri agrees with me, don't you?"

Dimitri had stopped by the door and stood with Vorana. "I... I think we need to question her. Cythera agrees Willow is a threat."

"How do you know for sure she's behind all of our problems?" Sorcha took a step back, uncertainty on her face as she tried to draw Gaian's attention to her.

"Stay out of this. I've been around enough bad people to recognize when someone is being dishonest. You're too naïve to see when there's a devious ghost right in front of you."

Sorcha's face paled. "I sense nothing bad coming from Willow. Just fear."

Gaian slid her a glare. "Perhaps it's time you went on another spa retreat. You've not been yourself for weeks."

"Sorcha is fine. Leave her alone." Zandra joined me in the room. "She's allowed to say what she thinks about this situation. And she agrees with us.

We let Willow have a chance to prove she's not guilty."

Gaian smirked. "Maybe you should take a break, too. This unofficial crime-fighting is going to your head."

"It's also going to yours," I said. "Who put you in charge of this investigation?"

"Don't like having your toes trodden on, huh? Of course not. You always think you're the boss around here," Gaian said. "Not this time."

"I have more experience than everyone in this room," I said. "And I've witnessed what happens when innocent people get accused of crimes they didn't commit."

"This ghost isn't innocent," Gaian said. "Sorcha, help me restrain her so I can get her in this pot."

Sorcha hesitated before slowly raising her hands and sparking her magic to life.

"Don't do this," Zandra said to her. "Gaian is pressuring you. If you think Willow is innocent, then stick up for her."

Sorcha's eyes narrowed. "He knows what he's doing."

"A few seconds ago, you were defending Willow," I said. "You know this is wrong."

"Do I? Or are you the ones putting pressure on me? Gaian always knows best."

A smirk twisted Gaian's face. "I sure do. And I know when trouble is in front of me. I'm never comfortable around ghosts. They shouldn't linger when their time has come to move on. Willow's been here for hundreds of years, trapped by a hex. That makes her unstable and dangerous.

She's behind our troubles. We get rid of her, and everything will resolve itself."

"One ghost can't be responsible for so much damage," I said. "Willow didn't do all of this."

"You're denying she's got power?"

"I... Maybe she once was powerful."

Gaian pursed his lips. "What do you know about her?"

I glanced at Zandra. "Nothing for certain."

"Go on. Reveal all. Or maybe you're in league with this ghost, and you don't want to share secrets about how helpful she's been."

I scowled at him. "You're sounding paranoid, Gaian. Or maybe you're deflecting. What would happen if we looked too closely at you? How many secrets would slither out?"

"You're wasting your time pointing the finger of suspicion at me. I hide nothing. And I know Angel Force has poked into my background and looked into all the gang members. Our aim is to do good. And when we find an individual, living or dead, who prevents that from happening, we deal with them."

"Just like you're dealing with Willow?" I said. "You don't let them prove their innocence. You shut them up and declare it a success."

"She's had her chance to talk, but instead she's chosen to hide. That's not my fault."

"I'm not hiding," Willow whispered. "I'm scared. Everything is unstable. It's all unsafe." Her frightened gaze drifted to Ember, who'd remained by Vorana's side.

"I'm sorry you were injured earlier," I said. "But you need to find the energy to tell us if you had a connection to Doctor and Mrs. Simister. Did you do something to Mrs. Simister while she was sleeping?"

"I promise, I didn't. I'm worried about all of you, so I wanted to make sure you were safe. When I came into your room, you were all asleep."

"We can't trust her," Ember said. "And I overheard what Finn told you about Willow's magic when she was alive. Willow can control the elements."

"You little sneak," Sage said. "Stop using your magic to snoop where it's not needed."

"That ghost is dangerous!" Ember jabbed a paw at Willow.

"No! Not anymore. I barely have the power to hold my form together. I focus on that, not making it rain or causing tornados." Willow's words trembled out of her mouth.

"We only have your word for that," Gaian said. "And it's not enough. Now we know what magic you possessed when you were alive, it shows you concealed important information from us."

"If she doesn't have access to that power anymore, it's not important," I said. "Leave her alone."

Gaian dismissed my comment with a grunt. "Willow, you can choose to go into this pot, or we'll drag you into it. You won't like that if we do."

Willow raised a shaking hand. "Please, don't make me go in there. I'll be alone and trapped."

"Then you'll know how we're feeling," Gaian said. "Once you're restrained and weakened, your power will fade. The barrier surrounding the inn will disappear, and we can get free."

"That won't work, because I'm not doing this. I know what it feels like to have no freedom. I'd never do that to anyone."

"Listen to her," I said.

"I'm done with this. We have our killer. Sorcha, restrain Willow while I shove her into this pot," Gaian said.

Sorcha didn't move.

"Don't make me ask again."

"Hey! You can't talk to her like that," Zandra said.

Vorana joined her. "Sorcha, ignore him. If you don't want to do this, you don't have to. Come be with us. We'll take care of you."

Top of Form

Sorcha scowled at them. "I'm with Gaian. Leave me alone." She thrust out her hands and twirled a restraining spell around Willow.

I'd intended to intervene, but when Sorcha cast the spell, her shirt sleeve rode up, revealing pale, glowing gremlin chaos symbols on her skin.

I stared open-mouthed at the discovery. What was she doing covered in those scandalous symbols?

"That's it. Hold her steady." Gaian lunged at Willow and swooped the pot over her several times. She wailed softly but put up no fight as the magic clamped its teeth around her and dragged her inside.

Gaian placed the lid on the pot and held it out, a triumphant smile on his face. "Case solved. One murderous ghost contained."

"Congratulations. You must feel so proud." I stood in front of Zandra, my hackles raised. My gaze flicked from Gaian to Sorcha. Were they both wearing gremlin chaos symbols on their bodies?

"Why shouldn't I? We'll soon be out of here." Gaian tucked the pot under one arm. "Don't be sour about this, Juno. I know you love to be in charge and solve problems in this town, but I'm happy to take up the slack. You should thank me for getting us out of this situation. I've just solved a double murder and got us free."

"You just accused and trapped an innocent ghost," I said. "The killer is still among us."

"She's here." Gaian patted the pot. "You'll see. Once Willow's destroyed, we can open the doors and leave. All we need is a quiet place to cast the destruction magic. Lila, what herbs do you have? It's not a spell I often use, so I'll need assistance."

Lila sucked in a breath. "No. This is my inn, and that means Willow is my ghost. I'll decide what we do with her."

Gaian's smile faded. "You can't think she's innocent, too. Don't believe Juno's lies."

"I didn't say she was innocent," Lila said. "But I need to be sure she's behind this before agreeing to have her destroyed. What if we make a mistake?"

"The only one making a mistake will be you if you don't see this through. Don't let the fake friendship she formed with you cloud your senses," Gaian said. "Why are you being so emotional about this?"

"I'm not! But I'm in charge here. You don't get to take over."

Gaian rocked back on his heels. "Be reasonable. We have no other option. Because of Willow's twisted magic, we're trapped. If we don't destroy her, who knows how long the barrier will take to come down? She'll weaken eventually, but it could take days. In case you've forgotten, there are two injured angels trapped and running out of food and water. If we don't get them out soon, they'll die. Do you want their deaths on your conscience?"

Lila scratched her forehead. "I need time to think."

"I understand this is a big responsibility, but don't let this weigh on your conscience. I'll exterminate Willow." Gaian passed the pot to Sorcha. He turned and gripped Lila's elbow. "You're not responsible for anything that happens here."

"This is my inn! My business! This doesn't feel right."

"You're not exterminating anyone," I said.

Gaian ignored me. "Take a few hours. Think about what'll happen if we don't destroy Willow. We can confine her in the pot and keep her in the attic out of everyone's way until you've made the right choice."

"No, not up there," Lila said. "It's unsafe. Some of the joists are rotten. I intended to get them repaired but ran out of money."

"You won't be able to fix them until you start generating an income. You can't do that until you've dealt with your ghost problem," Gaian said. "I know you're unhappy this place is haunted. You've done your best for Willow, and this is how she's repaid you. She's destroyed your business's reputation before you've shown how amazing this place could be."

"She doesn't deserve death as a punishment for scaring a few people and having a few bad moods," I said.

"We all know there's a gray area with ghosts," Gaian said. "They've already passed on from their corporeal form, and when they cause trouble to the living, there's always an option to remove them from circulation."

"Not by you," I said. "A decree like that comes from an official body. Or have you suddenly added unofficial ghost hunter to your resume?"

"I'll do whatever it takes to keep everyone safe," he said. "And that includes you, even though you don't appreciate it."

"I do need some time," Lila said. "Let's leave Willow in the cellar. Will that pot hold her?"

"She'll be good in there overnight," Gaian said. "And it'll give me time to make the destruction spell. Now Willow's trapped, we should see things improve. We'll keep trying the doors and windows. Soon, the barrier will weaken, and we can force our way out. Although Willow may put up a fight when we go up against her power."

"There was no fight in her after you'd whipped her with that spell," I said. "What did you use?"

"Nothing bad. She was faking it to get the sympathy vote. She'll soon realize she's been beaten. When Willow accepts there's no way back from this, there'll be no reason to keep us here." Gaian's smile held no warmth as he looked around the group.

"I'm not leaving you with that pot," I said.

Gaian raised his eyebrows. "Is that so? I suppose you want me to give it to you."

"We'll take it to the cellar and make sure Willow's comfortable and not under any risk of destruction."

"Juno, I'm flattered you think so highly of my skills, but even I can't conjure a destruction spell with the click of my fingers. It'll take me time to prepare. Willow won't be destroyed right away."

"Even so, Willow comes with us."

He flashed his teeth before the sharp expression morphed into a smile. "That's not happening. What's to say you won't let her out?"

"I'm willing to accept Willow's a suspect, so she can stay in that pot. But perhaps a few hours in there will prove to you she's not behind these troubles."

Gaian tilted his head. "How would that work?"

"When we remain trapped and the barrier stays strong, it'll show Willow's not involved."

"Or someone else gets killed," Zandra muttered.

"No more murders!" Lila said. "I can't handle it."

"Give me the pot," I said.

Gaian shook his head. "You're gonna have to take it from me."

It had been the excuse I'd been waiting for to wipe the smugness from his face. My fur bristled. "Hand it over."

His amused expression faltered for a second, but then he twirled a hand and sent a bolt of energy hurtling toward me.

I dodged it easily, leaping out of its path to redirect his blasts of power away from Zandra. My magic sparked to life, and I sent a large burst of flames at him.

Gaian deflected with a wave of his hand and blasted me with something sticky that stank of sour grapes. I leapt into the air, my claws extended, and raked them down his arm.

He stumbled back, clutching his bleeding arm, but he wasn't out of the fight. He pointed a finger at me and muttered an incantation, and suddenly, my limbs wouldn't move. I was frozen in place, helpless. But I wasn't giving up. I focused my ancient energy into a burst of knockback magic, sending Gaian flying. He crashed into the wall, and his hold over me broke.

I bounded over to him, my fangs bared, ready to bite something fleshy, but he held up his hand in surrender. "Enough, enough!"

I lowered my head, triumphant. "Hand over the pot."

He nodded and gestured at Sorcha, who held the pot to her chest, her eyes wide with alarm. "You fight well. We should team up sometime. We have a protest planned at a silver mine a few towns over. It's likely to turn ugly, so we need scrappy fighters on our side."

"Not a chance." I turned to Sorcha.

"Look out!" Zandra yelled.

I ducked as Gaian's magic buzzed past my ears, sizzling my fur.

"Stop!" Dimitri strode in between us. His wings blocked my view, so I couldn't see Gaian's irritating face, and they handily stopped the new spell Gaian had thrust at me.

Gaian growled his annoyance. "That cat is getting in the way of solving these murders."

"No more fighting." Dimitri's wings trembled, but he stood his ground. "I'll take Willow to the cellar and ensure the pot is left in a safe place."

"I should do it." Gaian waved away Sorcha as she tried to help him to his feet. "I caught the killer ghost."

"You sound petty," I said. "It's unbecoming."

"And you sound like a smug, privileged cat who thinks she's much more important than she really is."

"Enough! The pot?" Dimitri turned and held out a hand to Sorcha. "I want no more trouble. Everyone is tense and reacting badly to this situation."

After several disgruntled huffs, Gaian nodded at Sorcha, and she handed over the pot to Dimitri.

He nodded and folded one wing around it as if it was a precious egg he didn't want broken.

I stared intently at Sorcha, but I could no longer see the gremlin symbols on her skin.

"Let's get out of here before you try to take Gaian's head off again," Zandra muttered to me.

I nodded, turned, and left the room. Vorana, Ember, and Sage followed.

"So, that's it?" Vorana said. "Do you think this is over?"

I shook my head. "Far from it. We have a big problem. This mystery isn't solved. In fact, it's about to get a lot worse."

Chapter 17

Ticking clock

After leaving Gaian, Sorcha, and Lila, we waited for Dimitri and then followed him to the cellar. I was burning to tell everyone about the symbols I'd seen on Sorcha's arm but needed to ensure Willow was taken care of first.

"You don't have to worry. I won't let Gaian destroy her just yet," he said as he placed Willow's pot in the cellar as far from Doctor and Mrs. Simister's corpses as he could.

"That's comforting to hear. Although the just yet part of that sentence has me worried." I rested a paw on top of the pot. "I know this is scary, but stick with us. We'll get you out of there. I'll make sure Gaian comes nowhere near you." It shook under my paw, but I couldn't hear Willow. She must be terrified.

"I'll stand guard at the top of the cellar steps," Dimitri said. "I'll make sure no one interferes with Willow while we figure this out."

"I'd appreciate that." I headed back up the steps with the others. "Gaian has a flair for the dramatic, so I wouldn't put it past him to sneak down and destroy Willow just to prove a point."

"You don't like him much, do you?" Dimitri positioned himself by the closed cellar door.

"I'm rarely wrong about people. Behavior speaks volumes, while charming words are hollow. I was unsure about Gaian when I met him, but he made Sorcha happy, so I didn't interfere. But you should always trust your gut. It's the primitive part of you that is rarely wrong. It knows how to keep you alive and out of danger."

"What danger have you seen?" Dimitri's eyes were wide.

"Yeah, what's got you so worried? I know this isn't just about your distrust of Gaian. You saw something during the fight, didn't you?" Zandra stood with Vorana, Sage, and Ember.

"Sage, go sit at the bottom of the main staircase," I said. "It's crucial nobody overhears this."

She nodded and trundled off in her harness, positioning herself so she could see up the staircase and see us.

"Was anyone watching Sorcha when she cast that restraining spell around Willow?" I kept my voice low so we wouldn't be overheard.

They all shook their heads.

"When she held out her hand, her sleeve pushed up. Sorcha has gremlin chaos symbols on her skin."

Vorana's mouth fell open, and Zandra looked stunned.

"You're sure?" Vorana said. "Sorcha went through a phase of using temporary glowing tattoos. One day, she did half a sleeve of barbed wire. She thought it was hilarious when I asked if they were real."

"I've seen enough of those symbols to know what they were," I said.

"Sorcha is tied up with the gremlins messing with Crimson Cove?" Dimitri said.

I shook my head. "She'd never willingly get involved with something that would cause so much harm to the town she adores. Gaian has influenced her."

"Gaian's not a gremlin," Dimitri said. "He was telling me about how he uses his power to save the planet."

"You don't have to be a gremlin to use that kind of magic. You just have to be powerful. It won't be easy to create the symbols and imbue them with the chaos they demand, but it's possible. And there's a connection between those symbols showing up and Gaian's gang arriving in Crimson Cove. He's denied it and pretended he doesn't know what they mean, but I don't believe him."

"You think he's using them on Sorcha to keep her under control?" Anger flared in Zandra's eyes.

"I couldn't believe the way he talked to her. He dismissed her concerns and ordered her around like she was his servant," Vorana said. "The Sorcha I know and love would never stand for that."

"His happily ever after with Sorcha is a front," I said. "He's using her to make it look like he's a regular good guy. He dates one of the town's sweethearts while, in the background, he's preparing to ruin this place."

"Sorcha has changed so much," Vorana said. "I've been really worried about her."

"It's Gaian's fault," I said. "Sorcha innocently went into that relationship thinking she'd found her Mr. Right, but all this time, he's been using her to hide his true intentions."

"What are his true intentions?" Dimitri said.

"Looking at the chaos outside, it won't be anything good," I said. "Maybe Gaian wants his gang to take over Crimson Cove."

"A gang in Crimson Cove? That seems unlikely."

Zandra shook her head. "Not so much. Not long after we moved to the area, we discovered a group of magical thugs scaring the town. They had everyone under their thumb."

Vorana grimaced. "The Shadow gang. They were awful."

"We removed the problem, but that doesn't mean other gangs won't attempt to fill it," I said.

"Cythera's been looking into Gaian's gang," Ember said. "I overheard her say there's nothing bad about them. They do good for the environment. That's not criminal."

"You keep quiet," Sage said. "You weren't around when Crimson Cove was being terrorized. We want nothing like that to happen again."

"How are the murders here connected to Gaian's plan to take over?" Dimitri said. "Why kill two strangers? It doesn't make sense to me."

"Gaian didn't do it," Ember said. "He's a good guy. Maybe he's overprotective of Sorcha, but it's because he loves her. And he was in the bedroom all night when Mrs. Simister died, so it couldn't have been him."

"You were awake the whole time?" I asked.

"No! But I got up a few times to make myself comfy. Gaian was always in bed."

"Which means he could have snuck out."

"He'd never do that. But even if he did, I'd have heard the door," Ember said.

"You don't think it could be your friend, Sorcha, doing this, do you?" Dimitri said. "I'm not certain of her powers, but I'm aware she's a mix of vampire and something else. Could that be gremlin magic?"

"It's witch," Zandra said. "Sorcha is a vampire with a splash of witch magic thrown in to make her extra spicy, but she usually uses her vampire powers if she gets in trouble. And I've never heard her mention a link to gremlins."

"She hasn't a connection to gremlins," Vorana said. "And she loves Crimson Cove. She'd do anything to protect it. If she learned Gaian was planning to cause problems, she wouldn't allow it."

"Which means he had to exert his power over Sorcha by putting those symbols on her skin," I said. "She must be feeling so confused and helpless."

"What do the symbols do?" Dimitri said.

"Just a few on their own have limited power, but if you get enough of them in one space, the power grows exponentially. The symbols feed off chaos and get stronger. Their ability grows until they can basically do what they like. And as we can see by looking out the window, things have gotten worse since we've been here."

"That knowledge doesn't get us any closer to figuring out why Gaian would want Doctor and Mrs. Simister dead." Dimitri glanced at the main staircase. "Maybe I should talk to him."

"He'll deny any connection to the symbols or the chaos," I said. "Gaian is guilty."

"Slow down, Juno. We need evidence before we make such serious allegations," Dimitri said.

"Gaian didn't have any evidence when he trapped Willow," I said. "We should do the same to him."

"Let's take this one step at a time." Dimitri ran a hand through his perfect hair. "We can't restrain everyone."

"I'm not suggesting we do. Just Gaian. And he's the newest person in town. It has to be him."

"Other than Lila," Dimitri said after a short pause.

"Lila stood up for Willow," Vorana said. "She made sure Gaian didn't get his way and destroy her when he wanted to. She would have kept quiet if she was involved and needed someone to take the fall for the murders."

Dimitri opened his mouth, closed it, opened it again, then sighed. "I don't know about anyone else, but I'm lost. I need my manual. And I wish Cythera could see what was going on. She'd know what to do."

"Don't count on it," I muttered, although I shared Dimitri's frustration. The killer was here, but I couldn't pin them down.

I looked at Sage. "Talk us through what happened the night Mrs. Simister died. Did you see anything odd in your room? Gaian behaving strangely or having secret conversations with Sorcha?"

She shuffled closer, keeping an eye on the stairs. "Nothing like that, but I slept through. I guess I could have missed something."

"Like Gaian sneaking out to commit a murder?"

"Or Ember," Sage said.

"Stop blaming me," Ember snapped. "Or I'll whip that bony backside again."

Sage hissed at him.

"Ember, be polite," Vorana said. "You too, Sage."

"When we went to the guest bedroom to see what had happened to Mrs. Simister, you were bone-weary," I said to Sage.

She wrinkled her nose. "I take a while to get going in the morning."

"Because you're old," Ember said. "It's way past time you retired."

"That's not kind," Vorana said. "Sage is loyal and steadfast. I couldn't want for anything more in a familiar."

Ember lifted a paw and meowed piteously. "I only want the best for you."

"Of course you do, sweetie." Vorana scratched Ember's head gently. "But let's be nice to Sage. You two are practically siblings now we live together."

The second Vorana looked away from Ember, he scowled.

"You were more tired than usual," Vorana said to Sage. "So was I. I could barely get out of bed, and my feet felt like they were cased in concrete boots. I don't know why, but after I ate that piece of cake, I basically passed out."

"Cake? We didn't have cake for dessert," I said.

"When we went back to the room, Gaian had treats for everyone."

"Oh, sure. I forgot," Sage said. "He pulled out a box of cake for Vorana and Sorcha. Then he said, 'I suppose you want something too?' And he had a bag of cat treats! Not plant-based treats. These were the real deal. Full-on, intense, meaty goodness. He gave me ten treats."

"You're sure they were real meat? Gaian is always going on about how the fake meat substitutes taste like the real thing," I said.

"These were no dupe. Just like Vorana, I ate my treats and passed out."

"You passed out?" Zandra said.

Vorana nodded. "We were out like a light. I rarely sleep so soundly."

"Because of what was in the food," I said. "Gaian drugged you!"

"No! I ate some of them too," Ember said. "I was fine."

"I didn't see you eat anything," Sage said sharply. "You sniffed them, but that was all."

"Your eyesight is failing as well as your hearing," Ember said. "I definitely ate them."

"Now I think about it, it was weird," Vorana said. "One minute, I was talking to Gaian about a bathroom rota, and the next, it was morning. I don't even remember putting myself to bed."

"You did!" Ember said. "You were sleepy, though. I made sure you were tucked in and comfy."

"Are you in on this?" Sage hissed at Ember. "Did you know about the drugged treats?"

"What are you talking about, you paranoid old fleabag?"

"Ember! That's enough," Vorana said. "I didn't think anything of it. I was exhausted after the crazy day we'd had. Maybe... maybe there was something in that cake."

"And he fed it to Sorcha too?" Zandra's hands were clenched into fists.

"We both got a piece. I don't remember Gaian having any, though. He said he didn't have a sweet tooth."

My hackles lifted. "Gaian wanted you both quiet and out of the way. And he wanted to make sure Sage had her guard down so she wouldn't hear him when he snuck in and out of the room."

"He didn't do it!" Ember said. "I would have seen."

"You need to hush," Sage said. "You're too eager to support Gaian."

"Because I like the guy. He's always been good to me. Why are you trying to make him look guilty?"

"We need to see what Gaian is up to," I said. "We should search his room."

Vorana checked the time. "He's probably in there with Sorcha."

"Then we get him out and make sure the room stays empty so we can look around," I said, turning my attention to Ember. "It's time to prove your loyalty. Whose side are you really on?"

Chapter 18

Closing in

"Why do I have to be the one to put my life at risk?" Ember stomped his fluffy paws, his ears lowered.

"You're always bragging about how good your invisibility magic is," Sage said. "Now's the time to show us your astonishing abilities."

"But if Gaian is behind this, I'll be vulnerable!"

"You're sure he's not, so you have nothing to worry about." Sage tilted her head. "Or is there something you need to tell us?"

"Ember won't be vulnerable if he stays invisible," I said. "All you need to do is bang around in the attic until Gaian comes to look. Then we can search his room." I fixed Ember with a steely glare. "And this'll show us you're on our side and you want to help."

"I do! I just don't like seeing you chasing the wrong person. We're wasting time. We already have Willow trapped."

"Maybe Willow is the killer," I said, "but we must cover all the bases. If we destroy her and the murders keep happening, or we find ourselves still trapped, we'll have gotten nowhere."

"Other than having an unauthorized ghost vanquishing on our hands and conscience," Vorana said. "Sweetie, I know everyone is scared, but this would help. You're so good with your invisibility magic. I believe in you."

"I want to make you proud," Ember said.

"Then do this one thing." Vorana lifted Ember and kissed his head. "You're so brave. But be careful. If Gaian is involved, that makes him extremely dangerous."

"Ember's up to the challenge," Sage said. "He can achieve anything he sets his mind to."

Ember rested his paws over Vorana's shoulder and poked his tongue out at Sage. "I'll do it to make you happy."

"There's no need to show off, though," I said. "Keep Gaian distracted for as long as you can. Once he's left the bedroom and is in the attic, Zandra, you grab Sorcha. You have to get her out of that room."

"I can help with that," Vorana said. "I'll insist Sorcha speaks to us. I'll lay the guilt on thick and talk about how long we've been friends and how we need a resolution to this horrible situation. I know the real Sorcha is in there somewhere. She's a decent person, so she'll talk to us."

"Use whatever persuasion tactics you can to make sure that bedroom is empty," I said. "Once you and Zandra get her out of there, I'll sneak in with Sage, and we'll look around."

"I still don't know what you're looking for," Ember said. "It's not as if Gaian is hiding some giant gremlin manifesto under his pillow. We only meant to stop by to be polite and welcome Lila to town."

"Gaian brought a satchel in with him," I said. "I want to know what was in it."

"It was probably full of drugged treats for me and tainted cake for everyone else," Sage said.

"I keep telling you, you're looking at the wrong person," Ember said. "You'll feel embarrassed when Gaian is innocent."

"I'd rather be embarrassed and wrong than right but do nothing about it," I said. "Everyone knows what they need to do? Any more questions?"

Dimitri cleared his throat. "Shouldn't we clear this with Cythera?"

"We can ask for forgiveness later if it goes wrong," I said. "But every second counts."

His expression showed he was conflicted. "I... I should tell her. See what she thinks."

"You need to guard Willow and make sure nothing bad happens to her."

Zandra nodded. "We must make sure Gaian doesn't make a move and get rid of Willow. He'd never go up against such a strong member of Angel Force."

Dimitri puffed out his chest. "I won't let Gaian harm Willow."

"So, you agree with us? You stay here, and we'll clue hunt?" I tilted my head, masking my exasperation. This angel was incapable of making a simple decision.

Dimitri sighed. "I'll stand guard. But I must talk to Cythera as soon as possible."

"Let's get into position," I said. "Zandra and Vorana, we'll hide upstairs. We can watch when

Gaian leaves the bedroom, then once he's in the attic, you make your move."

Zandra nodded.

"Got it," Vorana said.

"Ember, it's time to get in that attic and stomp around," I said.

He huffed a few times, pausing to purr, when Vorana kissed his head again.

She set him on the floor. "You'll do an amazing job. Off you go."

We scurried up the stairs and into the bedroom we'd been sharing with Mrs. Simister, Cythera, and Finn. Ember slipped along the hallway and disappeared in a sparkle of magic. A moment later, there was a faint squeak as he pulled down the attic hatch. It was followed by loud bangs in the attic as Ember knocked things over.

The rest of us stayed by the bedroom door and peeked through a gap to see when Gaian would emerge.

"What's taking him so long?" Vorana whispered.

Sage grunted. "Maybe Ember tipped him off."

"Ember's been with us this whole time," I said. "He didn't have a chance to tell Gaian our plans."

We waited another couple of minutes as Ember danced around the attic like a clumsy fairy elephant on steroids.

"Someone needs to give Gaian a nudge," Zandra said. "I'll do it."

"Play it cool," I whispered.

"I always do." Zandra strode along the corridor and knocked on the bedroom door.

It was opened a few seconds later by Gaian. "What's up?"

"Can you hear those weird noises coming from the attic?"

"Sure. I figured it was Lila moving things around," Gaian said. "She said she had work to do now we'd caught the ghost. No problem in securing Willow in the cellar?"

"No problem. And I think Lila's downstairs, so it's not her." Zandra's tone sounded suitably worried. "I reckon there's an infestation up there."

Gaian sighed. "Nice. Another thing to deal with if we can't get out. You sure you don't want me to destroy Willow? When she's gone, we can get out and get on with our lives."

"Willow is innocent. But you should check out the noises," Zandra said.

"I should? Why?"

"Something does seem unhappy." Sorcha's quiet voice sounded from inside the room. "Maybe a possum got in. Those things do a lot of damage. They chew through wires and leave a mess," Zandra said.

"Go tell Lila. It's her inn, so it's her problem," Gaian said.

"Ever the gentleman," I murmured.

There were a few seconds of silence, but I knew my wonderful witch wouldn't back down.

"Lila's busy, so I don't want to bother her," Zandra said. "I guess I could go if you're scared of the dark. Or is it the rats giving you the chills?"

Gaian snorted. "I'm scared of nothing."

"I can come with you if you don't want to go alone," Sorcha said.

"Not a chance. I don't want you in some dusty old attic. Didn't Lila say something about the joists being rotten? You put your foot in the wrong place, and you'll go through the ceiling. You could break your neck," Gaian said.

"I'm lighter than you. And I'll be careful," Sorcha said.

"Stay here, babe. This is man's work."

I hissed softly. Zandra had just hit Gaian where it hurt.

"I won't be long." Gaian's footsteps echoed along the corridor as he headed to the attic.

Vorana slid out of the bedroom and hurried to join Zandra. Sage and I slipped out of the room too and hid around the corner, so we'd have easy access to Sorcha's room the second she left.

Zandra knocked softly on Sorcha's bedroom door again. "Hey. Come keep us company. The noises must be freaking you out. I almost jumped out of my skin when they started."

Soft footsteps approached the door, and it opened a crack. "Nothing freaks you out."

"This did. And with everything that's gone on here, I figured you wouldn't want to be alone."

There was a pause. "I thought you weren't talking to me."

"I'm talking to you! You just don't want to listen. And you've ignored me since you've been here," Zandra said.

Sorcha sighed. "It's easier that way. Gaian thinks you're trouble."

"Am I trouble too?" Vorana said. "I've missed hanging out with you. Come on, let's go to Zandra's room. We can catch up."

"I shouldn't. Gaian will be back soon."

There was more thumping overhead.

"He could be busy for a while," Zandra said. "Especially if that possum is giving him the run-around. Just five minutes."

"Okay. But just a few minutes. And I don't want to argue. Every time we see each other, that's all we do. It's exhausting."

"We can talk about the weather or... anything! You pick the topic," Zandra said.

Zandra and Vorana walked past, and Sorcha was right behind them.

I dashed out and grabbed the bedroom door with a paw before it fully closed. I held it open so Sage could fit through in her harness then eased it almost closed, tucking a ball of rolled-up socks against the frame so we could get out quickly if we were at risk of being caught.

"You take the left side of the room. I'll do the right," I said. "Look everywhere. Lift everything. We have to find something that incriminates Gaian."

"It won't take long," Sage replied, looking around the sparsely furnished room.

I hurried to the small brown chest of drawers beside the bed and hunted through each drawer. There was nothing in them. I looked under the bed. Nothing there too.

"Have you got anything?" I asked Sage.

"Sorcha's purse, but there's nothing unusual in it. Candy, lip balm, tissues, loads of receipts. How about you?"

I nudged open the built-in closet and found Gaian's cape hanging up. I grabbed the hem between my teeth and pulled it to the floor. I hunted through the pockets. "There are a few old bill slips and some money, but nothing else."

"There's nowhere else to look." Sage joined me.

"Where's his satchel? It's not in the closet, and I didn't find it under the bed. He didn't have it with him when he went to the attic."

We both looked up as several loud thumps overhead made the ceiling shake.

"What is that annoying kitten doing?" Sage said.

"His job. We can trust Ember. He wouldn't be helping if he was in on this symbol chaos scheme," I said.

"I'm still not convinced he's a good guy."

"Maybe he's not all good, but Vorana's been reprimanding him, so she's not letting him get away with too much bad behavior." I stood by the end of the bed and looked around again. There was still no sign of the satchel.

"Maybe Gaian left it downstairs," Sage said.

"We could look in the other rooms. He could have stashed it in another bedroom." I glanced at the ceiling. It had gone quiet. "If Gaian's given up his search for the mysterious possum, we need to get out of here. Let's try a couple of other rooms. Then we may have to admit defeat."

Sage jumped as there was another loud thud overhead, and her harness whacked a wooden wall panel. It creaked and fell away to reveal a small, dusty cubbyhole.

"That wasn't me! I barely touched it with my harness." Sage backed away from the damaged wall.

I hurried over and peered into the gloomy hole. "Well done, Sage. You found it!"

"I did? I mean, sure. What did I find?"

"Gaian's satchel!" I pulled it open and looked inside. It contained an almost empty box of cake and cookies and a bag of meaty-smelling cat treats. But what caught my attention was a glass jar of glowing white liquid.

"That's the food Gaian drugged us with. I recognize the smell of those treats," Sage said.

"Forget the treats. Look at this." I pulled the satchel out with my teeth and rolled it on its side. The glass jar fell out. "The gremlin symbols are painted in this liquid. This proves Gaian is behind all of it! He's been making the symbols."

The ceiling reverberated again, and we both jumped. There was a strangled yelp and then silence.

"Do you think Ember's been caught?" I pushed the satchel back into the cubbyhole, leaving the glass jar on the floor, and then shoved the panel back into place.

"That dumb kitten probably got distracted and dropped his invisibility magic. He's always doing that," Sage said.

"We need to warn Zandra and Vorana if Gaian's coming back." I grabbed the glass jar carefully between my teeth, and we hurried out of the room, kicking the rolled ball of socks back inside and allowing the door to close.

We raced back to Zandra's bedroom, and I scrabbled on the door with my paws so we'd be let in. No one opened the door. I thumped harder. Still no answer.

I placed the glass jar on the floor then leapt and caught hold of the handle, pulling it down. It was an old door, and the wood was heavy, so it took all my strength and a gentle blast of magic before it budged. I pressed my back paws on the door jamb and shoved.

Sage hurried into the room with the glass jar of glowing liquid in her mouth. I leapt nimbly onto the floor and entered behind her. There was no one in the room. A chair had been knocked over, and there was a shattered glass on the floor.

My heart did a triple beat of panic, and my throat tightened. "Zandra!"

Sage spat out the bottle. "What happened to them? If anyone has hurt Vorana, I'll—"

"What will you do? Gaian's voice interrupted us.

We spun around to discover him standing in the doorway. He had Ember perched on his shoulder, looking smug. But the sight that took my breath away and hit me in the heart with a razor-sharp stab was that Sammy and Tinkerbell were flanking Gaian.

Chapter 19

Friends reunited

"Sammy! What... what are you doing here?" My shock was undisguised as I took a step toward him. He looked wretched. His fur was dirty, his eyes glazed, and his tail drooped on the floor.

Gaian waggled a finger at me. "No closer. I see you've been poking around in places you shouldn't." His gaze was on the glass jar. "I knew the first time we met you'd be trouble."

"And I knew you couldn't be trusted." Sage violently hissed at Ember. "You're with him?"

Ember hissed back just as fiercely. "He's family. I'll always support him."

"Family? You're related?" I said, my gaze glued to Sammy.

Gaian smirked as Ember leaned against his cheek. "There's no need to go into details. I'm just here to take what's mine and ensure you get what's coming to you for attempting to ruin my plans."

"Sammy, listen to me," I said. "I don't know why you're with Gaian or what you're doing here, but it doesn't have to be this way. We used to be friends."

"You're wasting your time talking to them," Gaian said. "They don't want anything to do with you."

"They were the ones making the noises in the attic?" I said. "And when we first got here, we found muddy paw prints on the floor. Sammy and Tinkerbell have been here the whole time?"

"A work of great genius requires assistance," Gaian said. "I couldn't do this alone. I needed willing recruits, and I found some excellent ones lurking in the woods surrounding Crimson Cove. Sammy and Tinkerbell were happy to oblige me in taking this place down a peg or two before bending it to my will."

I tried to catch Tinkerbell's eye, but she wouldn't look at me. She looked in bad shape, the fur under her belly matted, and there was a large patch missing at the base of her tail.

"Hand over what belongs to me. Then you two are going somewhere you can't cause me any more problems," Gaian said.

"What have you done with Zandra and Vorana?" I snarled at him. "And where's Sorcha?"

"I did what I had to do to ensure their silence. Sorcha included. She was asking too many questions and not behaving like the good little girlfriend I required."

I snarled, a volcano of heat growing in my belly, but I forced my panic to stay in check. Zandra would be fine. She was one of the most powerful magic users I'd ever met. Gaian's sneakiness wouldn't fool her. And she had Vorana and Sorcha. Those three were formidable when riled.

Gaian petted Ember. "Settle yourself, Juno. No one else has to get hurt. Everything can still go to plan. You may even like to join in my fun. How about it?"

"We'll never side with you," Sage said. "Where's Vorana?"

His smile faded. "You'll obey me if you want your witches safe and left alive. Just do as I say and no one else needs to die."

I glowered at him, shimmers of magic sparking off my white fur. "You killed Doctor and Mrs. Simister?"

Gaian flashed his teeth. "Do we have a deal?"

"Never going to happen." I flipped in the air and hurled a shadow bolt spell at Gaian.

He countered with a fire blast. I deflected, and Sage destroyed it with a swipe of her paw.

I gestured with my chin for her to back off and keep an eye on Sammy, Tinkerbell, and Ember. Gaian's true power was dark, and no one needed to be tainted with it. I dodged and ducked as spells flew everywhere, ricocheting off the walls and sending furniture crashing to the floor.

Gaian was powerful, but his anger made him sloppy and his aim poor. We continued hurling spells back and forth, neither of us gaining the upper hand. He launched a lightning bolt my way, and I barely escaped, the fur crackling and burning across my head.

Ember jumped to the floor and joined Sammy and Tinkerbell, but none of them made a move to get involved. Were they waiting for a sign from Gaian to attack?

I hissed my rage at him, focused, and drew my ancient magic to the surface. I launched a radiant beam spell, and a wave of pure energy engulfed Gaian. He staggered back, his eyes widening in surprise. His skin undulated, like an incoming wave, the color shifting from pale pink to green. For a second, I didn't recognize the man before me. Then he raised his hand, and dark magic gathered around him.

Gaian launched a spell, a black bolt of energy that flew at my head. I ducked, but the bolt grazed my ear, leaving a singed patch of fur.

"You're good with the old magic." Gaian's voice dripped with contempt. "But you're not good enough to stop me. I've come too far. I will win." He launched another spell, and it hit me square in the chest. I stumbled back, the wind knocked out of me, but I refused to give up.

I channeled my energy into a single fire blast spell. I launched it at Gaian, and he went flying, crashing into the bed, his clothing and hair singed and smoking. But he wasn't done either. He rolled onto his feet and launched another spell at me.

We traded more blows, our spells colliding in mid-air and sending hot showers of sparkles around the room.

"You'll regret challenging me," Gaian growled, as he tossed another spell.

I ducked and rolled, coming up behind him. I launched a spell of my own, another blast of fire that singed his shirt. He whirled around, his eyes blazing with fury.

He raised his hand, and a sticky, dark magic gathered around him. Gaian was about to unleash something grossly powerful, and it was aimed at me.

"What's going on?" Sorcha stumbled out of the attached bathroom. She was holding one side of her head, and blood trickled down her cheek.

"You're a hard creature to keep down," Gaian snarled. "Why do you have to be so difficult?"

She blinked several times. "Did you do this to me? I don't remember—"

"You should remember nothing, you irritating hybrid. I've lost track of the number of drugged meals I've forced down your neck, yet you still keep asking questions. Just obey me." He slammed a spell into Sorcha's chest, and she fell back and hit the wall.

"Why are you doing this? I... I care for you. I love you." She rubbed her chest as his magic sparked over her. "Gaian, tell me what's going on. Is... is that Sammy and Tinkerbell?"

Gaian grunted his disgust. "You pathetic being. I never wanted you. I wanted access to what you had."

"Leave her alone." I jumped in front of Sorcha. "You've hurt her enough."

His top lip curled. "I'm done with her, anyway. This is almost over."

Tears pricked Sorcha's eyes. "Why are you fighting Juno and Sage? And what are you doing with Tinkerbell, Sammy, and Ember?"

"I thought you were just pretty and dumb. An easy mark," Gaian said. "If I'd known you were so nosy and annoying, I'd never have bothered with you. I made a mistake picking you to get me an in to this town. Maybe I should have targeted Vorana. She seems almost as lonely and miserable as you. And she's a better cook."

A strangled noise of confusion slipped from Sorcha's lips, and the tears she'd been holding back slid down her cheeks.

I growled at him. Sorcha was my friend, and Gaian had just done the unthinkable by breaking her heart so callously.

Gaian smirked, swiped his hands to the right, and I was lifted off my paws and pinned to the ceiling. I twisted and howled as his prickly, tar-like magic held me in place.

Sage coiled and threw herself at Gaian.

Sorcha screamed as Gaian grabbed at Sage, but she was fast and whacked him around the head with her metal harness several times, ricocheting off him and hitting him in the face with a wave of purple magic.

Gaian gagged and dropped to his knees. Ember ran up to him, but he waved him away as he gasped in air.

"Gaian, you need help." Sorcha staggered to her feet and took a step toward him.

"Don't go near him!" I yelled.

Her face was full of confusion and sadness as her chin wobbled. "He told me he wanted to marry me. He said he'd make plans for us to be together forever."

"Gaian lied to you to get what he wanted!" Gaian's magic still had me pinned, my face smooshed against the ceiling and my body growing uncomfortably warm.

"Don't listen to Juno. Something evil has possessed her. Sage, too. They're dangerous." Gaian tried to stand but failed and remained on his knees. "Help me, babe. I know you want to."

Sorcha dashed to his side, her blind devotion making her forget the things he'd just said to her and how cruelly he'd used his power against her.

Gaian grabbed Sorcha around the throat and yanked her in front of him. His chest heaved in and out. "Make any more moves against me, and I'll kill her."

The terror and broken-hearted agony in Sorcha's eyes made me pause in my efforts to break his spell and obliterate him. I couldn't risk Sorcha's life.

Gaian smirked as Sorcha twisted in his grip. "Better. You're seeing sense. Maybe I'll have use for you in my new kingdom."

"We'll never work for you," Sage said, her path to Sorcha blocked by Ember, Sammy, and Tinkerbell.

"You'll work for me, or you'll die," Gaian said. "Those are the options."

"We don't accept those options," I said. "We choose to obliterate you."

"Remember, your witches' lives are at risk. And I know you'll do anything to protect them. Ember is always telling me how protective Sage is of Vorana."

"I'll deal with you later." Sage growled at Ember.

Ember giggled. "You've got no idea what's going on. I made you think I was the perfect replacement, while you stupidly let me into your life. You gave your witch up so easily. It was barely a fight."

"You've been working with Gaian all this time?" I watched Sorcha closely, but Gaian wasn't hurting her, just holding her in front of him as a shield. Coward. I kept working on the binding spell, feeling it loosen as Gaian focused on keeping Sorcha under control.

"I've been gaining your trust, making sure you lowered your barriers and were distracted so you couldn't see what was going on. It worked." Ember swiped a paw at Sage.

"You did an excellent job," Gaian said. "Our family will be proud of us when we declare victory."

"Your family?" I said. "How are you related?"

Gaian bared his teeth. "You'll soon see how far I'll go to prove to them I'm good enough. Now, move. I need you out of my way while I unleash the new version of Crimson Cove."

"We're going nowhere until you tell us where our witches are and that they're safe," Sage said.

"They're safe, after a fashion. They're still breathing. And if you want to see them, then you'll come with me. Or do I need to set an example with the delectable Sorcha and show you I mean business?" Gaian squeezed her neck, and she squeaked.

"Kill Sorcha and I'll ruin you," I said.

"You can try. But I have your witch, and she's injured. Don't familiars die if their bonded magic user is killed? Hmmm... maybe I should test that theory on Zandra."

"Take us to them. Now!" Murderous hatred boiled my blood and made me pant. I had to be with my witch and ensure she was okay.

"They're in the attic. You go ahead of us." Gaian released the binding spell, and I dropped to the floor. He stood and stepped out of the room, dragging Sorcha with him. Ember jumped back on his shoulder, while Sammy and Tinkerbell flanked him.

I stared hard at Sammy as I passed him, but he wouldn't look at me. His head was down and his breathing labored. He looked like he was on his last legs.

"Keep moving," Gaian said. "Time is not on my side, which means Zandra and Vorana are at even more risk if my plan fails."

"Where are Dimitri and Lila?" Sage whispered to me. "They must have heard the fight."

"I have an idea about that," I muttered back.

"No conspiracy whispering," Gaian said. "Head to the attic stairs and get up there. Tick tock, the witches are almost dead."

We sped up, and I assisted Sage in dragging her harness up the steps.

"Keep going. You'll find exactly what you want up there." Gaian stood at the bottom of the stairs.

I shoved open the attic hatch and peered through. Vorana lay on her side, her hands and feet bound, and a gag in her mouth. Her eyes were closed, but I could see she was breathing. Zandra sat next to her. She was also tied and gagged, but at least she was awake.

I looked over my shoulder at Gaian, a tsunami of hatred pouring through me. "You'll be sorry you ever met me and my witch."

"If you say so. Don't you want to make sure she's okay? I had to hit her hard before she stayed down." Gaian sneered at me.

Ember hissed and thrust out a spell that whacked me in the back.

I jumped into the attic and hauled Sage up after me.

"You, too," Gaian said.

Sorcha inhaled sharply. "No! Gaian, this is a mistake. Maybe you're the one possessed. We can get you help. Make you better. You don't mean this."

"Get up those stairs!"

Sorcha cried out before she appeared and shuffled into the attic. The hatch slammed shut behind us, and a wave of fetid magic crossed the room, suggesting we'd been sealed in. But I didn't care about that. I dashed to Zandra and tugged the gag out of her mouth.

She heaved in a breath. "It's Gaian! He's behind all of this."

I nodded as I licked her face and checked for injuries. "I know. We found a jar of liquid he's been using to make the gremlin chaos symbols. He's working with Ember, Sammy, and Tinkerbell."

"I couldn't believe it when I saw them. Why are they involved with him?"

"He's got them under some kind of compulsion spell," I said. "Sammy and Tinkerbell look sick. Gaian's not taking care of them."

We froze as the attic hatch opened again. A second later, Sammy and Tinkerbell were tossed inside and the hatch sealed.

I stood in front of my witch, protecting her, and Sage did the same for Vorana. We both growled so low and deep, the floor twitched beneath our paws.

I stepped forward, my hackles raised and teeth bared. I'd do everything in my power to protect Zandra. And if that meant killing Sammy, then so be it.

Chapter 20

The pieces connect

I snarled at Sammy as I swirled a shimmer of hot red shield magic around Zandra and Sorcha. "Stay away from us. You put one paw wrong, and I'll obliterate you."

Sage stood in front of Vorana, a similar magic shield surrounding them. She hissed her agreement, her fur a magnificent, frizzy display of power.

Tinkerbell staggered to her paws and stood in front of Sammy. He was barely moving as he lay on his side. "Leave him alone."

"You're both working with Gaian," I said. "That makes you our enemies."

"What choice did we have?" Tinkerbell glanced back at Sammy.

"Every choice! Ever since I've known you, you've enjoyed causing trouble, and now you've dragged Sammy into your murky mix of malice. I'm warning you—"

"What? We had nothing left to lose. We had no magic user to bond with, no friends, and then

Sammy got sick. None of you cared. None of you came to find him. You were so happy in your little bubbles of perfection that we were ignored. We had to find somewhere we'd fit. Someone who wanted us and saw we had value."

"There are no excuses for what you've done. You've always been a troubled cat," I said.

"It's not her fault," Sammy whispered. "Tinkerbell hasn't been as lucky as you."

My gaze flicked to Sammy. My heart clenched, but I wouldn't back down. He'd been sent into the attic with Tinkerbell to destroy us.

"Ignore him. I can look after myself," Tinkerbell said. "Sammy's a soft touch. I sold him a sob story so I wouldn't be alone and had someone with me, so we'd look out for each other if things went bad. We take care of each other."

"Working with a conniving gremlin cult is hardly taking care of yourself," I said.

"I knew you wouldn't understand when you realized we were involved," Tinkerbell said. "I kept telling Sammy we should cut our losses and run while we could. But he wouldn't listen. He's as obsessed with you as ever."

"He... he is?"

"Now we're in this mess!" Tinkerbell hissed her anger. "Trapped in this inn while Gaian and Lila put their final plan in place."

"Lila?" Zandra said. "She's involved, too?"

I backed up until I sat on Zandra's feet, testing our connection, happy to feel it strong and healthy. I kept the shield spell in place, but neither Tinkerbell nor Sammy made any move to attack. "When I searched Lila's office with Dimitri, there were no personal effects. Not a single picture of family members or friends, and no sign of her hobbies. It was as if she'd created the office from a bland template so as not to raise suspicion she was hiding something."

"She also had Doctor Simister's briefcase, didn't she?" Zandra said. "But how is Lila involved?"

"You're not as smart as you make out," Tinkerbell said. "This inn is their base. Lila is as mixed up in this mess as Gaian is."

"You can't trust Lila," Sammy said. "She's not as nice as she makes out."

"I saw Lila and Gaian whispering together, and I wondered if something was going on between them," I said. "Gaian seemed familiar with her."

"Familiar! You thought they were having an affair?" Sorcha said.

"I was unsure what to think. I've never trusted Gaian."

"Why didn't you tell me?"

"I had little evidence to go on and didn't want to worry you until I knew for sure," I said. "And, given your frame of mind, I knew you wouldn't believe me."

Sorcha huffed out a breath but nodded.

"Lila also gave Gaian the drugged food to keep Vorana and Sorcha under control, didn't she?" I asked Tinkerbell.

"And Sage." Tinkerbell smirked. "She always was greedy, so that was no challenge."

Sage scowled at her. "I may be greedy, but at least I'm not a disgusting betrayer."

"Who am I betraying? My bonded witch? Oh, I don't have one of those. My friends? Nope, none of them, either. My family? All dead." Tinkerbell shrugged a thin shoulder. "It's just me."

"You're betraying your home," I murmured.

Tinkerbell snarled at me. "I don't have one of those. I've never been accepted in Crimson Cove."

A flicker of sympathy cut through my rage, but I wouldn't let Tinkerbell deceive me again. The time for kindness was long gone.

"The inn is a cover for the gremlin cult?" Vorana said.

I nodded. "It makes sense they needed somewhere to hide while they put their plan into action. Gaian arrived first with his group of fake eco-warriors. They laid the groundwork for the cult by placing symbols around the town. I'm assuming they used you, too, to do that?" I said to Sammy and Tinkerbell.

"You were never meant to see me at the Blood Moon Festival," Sammy said. "I intended to run, but I knew you needed help to find a suspect, and I'd seen where he'd hidden. I couldn't abandon you. Not again."

Tinkerbell turned and boxed his ears. "Idiot! I knew that was a mistake. Once Juno gets her teeth into something, she never lets go. I told you she'd be watching for any sign you were lurking around."

"Juno needed me. And I wanted to help her." He turned his sorrowful gaze to me. "I know I've been different, but that's not my fault."

"Whose fault is it?" Sage said. "You were the one who turned into a giant jerk and rejected Juno. She's been heartbroken. She pined for you for ages."

I gestured for her to stop, my body hot with embarrassment. "I have missed you. And I wondered if you were lending me a helping paw when you showed me where that suspect was hiding."

"It was a stupid moment of weakness," Tinkerbell said. "One he regrets, don't you, Sammy?"

Sammy closed his eyes and refused to answer.

"Getting back to the fact we're trapped in an attic with a gremlin cult about to unleash bedlam on Crimson Cove, we should focus on the most immediate problem." Zandra rested a hand on my head, her gentle touch soothing the ache in my heart.

I took a moment to calm myself. I had a tornado of tumultuous emotions weaving inside me. I felt sick, panicky, and broken-hearted that Sammy was in such a desperate situation. I wanted to heal him, help him, let him know I still cared, but this wasn't the time.

"Give me a moment. I must assist my witch." I broke the bindings on Zandra's ankles and wrists, a nasty tingle of magic surrounding them. "What happened?"

"I happened," Sorcha whispered. "I attacked Zandra and Vorana. There's... something horribly wrong with me. I tried to bite them. Then I hit them with magic."

"And then Gaian appeared." Vorana pressed her lips together.

"It's not you. It's the symbols on your arm," I said to Sorcha. "When did Gaian start putting them on you?"

"Symbols?" Sorcha's eyebrows lowered, and she pulled up the sleeve of her shirt. Sure enough, there were half a dozen gremlin chaos symbols faintly glowing in the gloom. "What are these?"

"They're how Gaian controls you." I cast a warning look at Tinkerbell and Sammy then moved closer to Sorcha. "Gaian isn't the good guy he claims to be."

She was quiet for several seconds. "I care about him. We've been planning our future. He must be unwell, saying all those terrible things. He wouldn't use me. I wouldn't be stupid enough to fall for someone like that, would I?"

"Not while you're your usual awesome self, but you've changed since Gaian came on the scene," Zandra said. "I tried to talk to you about him a few times, but you wouldn't listen."

"Why would I? You were jealous of my happiness," Sorcha said. "You didn't like that Gaian took my attention from you."

"That's partly true," Vorana said with some reluctance, "but we were more worried that he was manipulating you into someone you didn't want to be."

Sorcha scowled and looked away. "I don't know what to believe. I was so sure about him. Everything he said made sense."

"Sorcha, Gaian is tainted with dark gremlin magic." I shuffled closer to her. "And I believe he's also part gremlin. When we were fighting, I saw his disguise slip. He's using immensely powerful magic to ensure no one sees his true form. That magic has a dark tint to it. You've been spending so much time with him that some of that darkness would have rubbed off on you."

"That can't be true. He said he'd always look after me."

"Until you've served your purpose," Tinkerbell said. "The guy is a jerk. He promised us everything, and now he's done this! Locked us here with you, our enemies. We should have gotten out while we had the chance." She glared at Sammy.

Zandra moved closer and tentatively touched Sorcha's arm. "We need to get those gremlin symbols off you. Whilst they're on your skin, they'll mess with your thoughts."

Sorcha scratched at the symbols with her nails. "Are you sure? I don't remember Gaian putting these on me."

"What's the last thing you do remember?" I asked. "You said you attacked Zandra and Vorana."

"We were chatting. It was kind of awkward, but a part of me was glad they'd reached out. Then Gaian appeared with Ember, and he wanted to know what was happening. We were all talking, and I got a pain in the back of my head. That's all I remember. I woke in the bathroom and heard Gaian arguing with Juno."

"It was like Gaian flipped a switch in your mind," Zandra said. "He told you to attack us."

Sorcha shook her head. "No! He wouldn't."

"He did," Vorana said. "You went for Zandra first, while Gaian fought with me. He stunned me with a spell then helped you with Zandra."

"I was so shocked." Zandra touched the back of her head. "He surprised me. I hit the floor and then saw him whack you and drag you into the bathroom. I must have blacked out for a minute because, when I came to, we were in here."

Sorcha chewed on her bottom lip. "I'd never hurt either of you."

"You've been under the influence of those gremlin symbols for a while. And they were on your arm before that fight," I said. "I saw them when you were trapping Willow. Gaian must have worried he was losing control of you."

Sorcha stared at her arm and sighed. "I should have known it was too good to be true. It felt too perfect. Was it really all a lie?"

"Given the situation we're in, you can assume yes," Zandra said. "Sorry."

Sorcha's eyes filled with tears, but she pushed back her shoulders and nodded. "Get these symbols off me. No one makes a fool out of me or my friends and gets away with it."

"That's my Sorcha." Vorana smiled at her.

It took several attempts using a counter-chaos spell and muttered grumbles from Zandra before all traces of the symbols were removed from Sorcha's skin. During that time, Tinkerbell and Sammy hadn't muttered a word or made any move to attack.

Once everyone was more comfortable and settled, we returned to the issue of being trapped in the attic.

"We can't trust Lila to help, since she's involved," Vorana said, "but where's Dimitri? The last time I saw him, he was guarding the cellar. Why didn't he help when he heard the fighting?"

"Maybe Lila or Gaian got to him," Zandra said. "Dimitri could be stuck in the cellar with Willow and the bodies."

"When we get out of here, we need to free Finn and Cythera," I said.

"How?" Zandra said. "We've been trying to get them out ever since they were trapped in that room."

"We'll find a way." I glanced at Sammy. Would he be willing to help? Did he have the strength to do so?

"Why did Gaian and Lila kill Doctor and Mrs. Simister?" Vorana asked.

"I believe they're also gremlins," I said.

"How do you know that?" Zandra said.

"When Mrs. Simister tried to get out of the bedroom, she was injured, and her hand turned green. I thought it was a side effect of the barrier spell, but it was because, for a moment, her disguise failed. Just like Gaian's disguise failed when we fought. Mrs. Simister hid her hand and said it was nothing, but it must have been painful. She couldn't risk getting it treated in case we figured out she wasn't who she said she was."

"That wouldn't have convinced me they were gremlins," Vorana said.

"There were also scratches and marks on the wood," I said. "Gremlins love to sharpen their claws and teeth on wood. They're like cats. We can never resist a tempting piece of wood to score our territory marks. And then there were their appetites."

"They did eat a lot at the buffet," Zandra said.

"And their table manners left a lot to be desired. Gremlins are notoriously greedy, and they love treat foods. I lost count of the number of plates Mrs. Simister ate."

"I didn't. And between the two of them, they ate a giant meat pie I had my eye on," Sage said.

"Why did they come to the inn?" Vorana said.

"To help Gaian and Lila?" Zandra shrugged. "But then something went wrong?"

"They must have been enemies." I looked at Tinkerbell and Sammy. "Perhaps you can fill in this gap."

Tinkerbell looked away.

Sammy heaved in a breath. "I don't know why the Simisters were here or what their gremlin rank was, but Gaian was angry about their visit. I overheard him say to Lila they needed to be dealt with quickly, so I guess they weren't friends."

"Gaian worked with Lila to figure out a way to kill them," I said. "Maybe the Simisters threatened to expose their plan, or they weren't happy with their progress in infiltrating Crimson Cove. Whatever the reason, they had to be disposed of."

"My lying boyfriend is also a murderer." Sorcha shook her head. "I sure know how to pick them."

"Now we know who's behind this," Zandra said, "what do we do next?"

I rested a paw on her knee. "We get justice."

"And revenge," Sage said.

I hissed. "And just a touch of revenge for what they did to our witches."

Chapter 21

Making a plan

We hunted every inch of the attic, looking for a weakness in the magic or a way out. I'd peeked through a tiny gap in a joist to see it was dark outside. It felt like the early hours of a new morning.

"Things still sound chaotic out there." Sage joined me and tugged at a sticky cobweb stuck to her whiskers. "But it's no worse than the last time I looked, so the chaos makers still have work to do."

"They're most likely gathering their army of chaos gremlins so they can achieve victory," I said. "Which we can't allow. We have to get out of this attic."

"If we use magic to blast our way out, it could kill our witches," Sage said. "Vorana got burned when she tried the hatch."

"And Zandra's hair caught on fire when she attempted an unlock spell." The stench of frazzled hair still hung in the air. "We can't let them help anymore. We're powerful enough without them. If we join forces, we can use brute magical force to get out of here."

Sage drew in a slow breath. "You think you can survive that amount of magic? The kickback could tear us apart."

"The odds aren't in our favor, but I'd rather I was injured than Zandra."

"We're not just talking injured, though, are we?" Sage looked over at Zandra, Vorana, and Sorcha. They sat together, their heads bent close. I was certain they were talking about how to escape from the attic. We'd tested the barrier trapping us repeatedly and had been given a warning each time. Those warnings would get more painful and lethal if we kept probing.

"The reward will be worth it."

Sage succeeded in removing the sticky web from her whiskers, getting it stuck to her right paw instead. "I'd lay down my life for Vorana. I don't want to leave her, but I feel okay about doing this now she knows the truth about Ember. I'd never leave her with that sneaky little liar."

"Sorry I doubted you about him. I can't figure out why he's affiliated with Gaian. The family connection has me stumped."

"If we ever get out of here, we'll ask him," Sage said. "Then I'll take a leaf out of your book and obliterate him."

"He had us all fooled."

"Not me. But I let my fear of not being good enough for Vorana cloud my judgment. I saw a young, powerful, skilled familiar in waiting, and he seemed perfect for her."

I turned to my friend. "Sage, you're perfect for Vorana. You keep each other strong and, most importantly, you keep each other blissfully happy. Of course, when a sad-faced pathetic-looking kitten showed up on her porch, she took him in and cared for him. But her love for you is infinite. If you ever left her, she'd be heartbroken."

"And I get that now! I am good enough for her." Sage glanced back at Vorana then nodded. "If sacrificing myself to get everyone free is what it takes, then it's worth it. Although... maybe neither of us has to perish."

"I hope we don't. What are you thinking?"

"I'm thinking you."

"You want me to break us out on my own?"

Sage wrinkled her nose. "We do this together, but you need to stop holding back. I know you've found several pieces of your old magic, and I can sense your power is shifting. I have a feeling you're changing, too." She looked at my tail stump.

"We all change. But I don't trust that magic. It doesn't behave as I need it to. And it won't behave until I've got it all back."

"I disagree. You don't believe in yourself. You're worried you'll hurt someone, or yourself, or a spell will go wrong and you'll look like an idiot. Who cares? Look stupid. Test what you've got. Make it fit to the new version of you."

"It's not just that." I stared at Zandra. "If it was only me, I'd have no issue with testing my boundaries."

"You think Zandra will look at you differently when she learns the truth?" Sage said.

If I had eyebrows, I'd have arched one. "You don't even know the truth about me. It may change your mind when you learn exactly what I was."

"I've got a good idea. And I know you'll tell me everything when the time is right. But what I'm not willing to wait on is you being too fearful to use what you have when we so desperately need it."

"There are no guarantees we'll break out, even if I unleash everything I've got."

"I'm not asking you to offer that guarantee." Sage nudged me with her head. "But I can't do this alone. I need you by my side. And I need you to bring everything you've got in that old weird magic-smelling trunk of yours. If you hold back, we won't get free. Then Gaian and his twisted gremlin cult family will win."

I focused on Zandra again. She was in a heated discussion with Vorana, and they weren't discussing make-up tips. They were plotting the same thing as us. A way to get us out. I wouldn't risk my witch's life. But if I did this, if I unleashed the ancient power inside me, she'd know what I'd been hiding since we formed our familiar bond. It would change things. Maybe that change would be bad. Maybe Zandra wouldn't want me anymore.

"Zandra's an excellent witch. She's had her share of troubles and changes, too. She'll understand why you held back," Sage whispered.

"What if this breaks our bond?" I gulped against the lump in my throat. "I've never felt such a strong, pure bond before. I tried so many times with other magic users, and it always felt wrong. Yet, the second I met Zandra, I knew she was the one for me. If that's taken, I won't survive."

"None of us will survive if that gremlin cult takes over the town. They won't let us live. We know too much. And we'll keep fighting them. The second they're done getting the last pieces of their plan into place, they'll come for us."

"So whichever choice I make, I'll lose Zandra?"

Sage swatted me with a hard paw. "That's your fear talking. I know about that, since I've lived with it ever since I foolishly allowed Ember to come into our lives. It'll eat you up from the inside if you let it take hold. Trust your witch. She'll be there for you, no matter what you say to her."

I wasn't ready for Zandra to know the truth about me, but Sage was right. I had to trust myself if we were to save Crimson Cove and all the people we loved.

"I can help." Sammy inched his way across the floor, sliding on his belly and using his paws to drag himself along. "If you need to blast your way out without Zandra seeing what you're doing, I can distract her."

"You stay out of this," Sage said. "We don't trust you."

Sammy cringed back. "You're right not to. I am sorry, though. Ever since I got hit with that sleeping potion at Grace Laker's house, I've not felt right. My thoughts have been muddied and confused."

I stared at him with wide eyes. "You've not been feeling well since then? Why didn't you tell me?"

"I didn't know anything was wrong! And that werewolf said it was an old potion with no power. But this weird, paranoid feeling crept over me and got worse and worse."

"Sammy, if we let you help us, can we trust you to do the right thing?" My heart pitter-pattered as I saw the war going on inside him.

"You're making a mistake," Sage said.

"If a werewolf potion has messed with Sammy's head, it's not his fault," I snapped. "I can see he wants to change."

"I do! I don't feel myself, and I need help. I can't keep feeling like this, and I only pushed you away because I knew there was something wrong with me. I never meant to get tangled up with that demon or with Gaian, but I'm drawn to chaos and darkness. When I'm in the middle of instability, I feel... good."

"What was in that werewolf potion?" I asked.

"Not rosewater and fairy toots if it's making him feel like that," Sage said.

"I need to speak to Grace and find out what she had stored in her antiques collection. She concealed the truth, and Sammy got sick."

"You can't face off with a high-ranking werewolf while we're stuck in here," Sage said. "We need to move now before our witches get injured. Focus on the gremlins, not the werewolves."

I glanced at Tinkerbell. She'd retreated to one corner and had her back to us. "What about your new best friend?" I said to Sammy.

"I told her I want to help you. She said it was my funeral and has ignored me ever since."

I reached out and gently touched Sammy's face with a paw. He flinched but then stilled. The magic covering him was disturbingly cold and sticky. It felt like I was trying to hold a handful of tar spiked with grit. But I didn't pull back. I wanted him to know I still cared and would look after him.

"I'll pretend I'm sick. I'll ask for Zandra's help," Sammy said.

"You don't have to pretend," I whispered. "I'm sorry. I didn't realize what was wrong with you."

"How could you, when I didn't know? I only found out when I went back to the Laker house and asked her about the potion."

"What did Grace tell you?"

"She denied it at first, but when she saw how ill I was, Grace let me in and made a few calls. Once she was done, she said she was sorry. I had to get my affairs in order and say goodbye to the people I cared about."

"So, instead of doing that, you turned to the dark side?" Sage said.

"That dark side found me. It kept me alive."

"Oh, Sammy!" I sniffed his fur. He stank like an unwashed soccer sock lost in the depths of a clothes hamper for a month.

"I can do it! They'll be distracted looking after me, then you and Sage blast the attic hatch open. But be careful. Gaian has been dabbling with nasty dark magic. It gains strength from fear and pain. You can't show you're afraid, or you'll strengthen it."

"I'm determined to get us free. Fear won't defeat us. Thank you, Sammy."

"I should thank you. You had every right to destroy me the second you saw me, but instead, you still want to help. I don't deserve that."

"That's exactly what you deserve. You're an excellent cat."

"Enough soppy stuff," Sage said. "Let's get out of here and destroy Gaian, Lila, and Ember."

I assisted Sammy to his feet and then gently pushed him toward Zandra, Vorana, and Sorcha. He put on an impressive performance, staggering from side to side and groaning as he weaved toward them.

Of course, my wonderful witch was instantly on her feet and gathering him into the fold of witches so they could help him. The second their backs were turned, I closed my eyes and dug in deep to the old magic inside me. It bubbled and twisted, sensing I was drawing on every ounce of ancient energy and demanding its service.

Sage's paw thudded against my side. "We'll do this together. We'll share a connection. Take what you need from me."

I opened my eyes and looked at her. "You sure you can handle that?"

Sage snorted. "You'll be surprised at what I can handle."

"Never. I've never underestimated you. Together, we can do this."

A quick glance at Zandra showed she was occupied with caring for Sammy. I scurried to the attic hatch with Sage. We placed our paws on the wood and flooded it with magic. The hatch bucked under the spell, straining at the hinges and writhing across the joists.

"Juno! What are you doing?"

I barely heard Zandra's voice, since I was so focused on breaking us out.

"We need more time and more power," Sage said. "Hurry!"

I dove deeper into my magic. I was still holding back, but I couldn't afford to anymore. I thrust more magic into the spell. The wood screeched, and sparkles of power lit the gloom in the attic and swirled around us.

An unearthly howl nearly pierced my eardrums, and I was tossed into the air with Sage. Zandra caught me before I thudded to the floor, my limbs shaking, and my skin feeling on fire. She held me close against her chest, her heart racing. "You could have been killed trying that without me."

"Did it work? Did the hatch open?" I saw stars and blackness blinked in the corner of my vision.

"Almost. The barrier's still in place, though." She stroked her hands over me several times. "Juno, we need to work together. You can't shut me out."

I gazed at Sage. She was being cradled by Vorana, her limbs twitching and fur smoking. Vorana caught my eye, her expression fear-filled and tense. "She's alive. Just."

"As wonderful as you both are and as much as you want to protect us, we're better when we work together." Zandra kissed my head several times. "I know you're special. I knew it the second we met. I also know there's a good reason you hide how much power you have from me. But you must stop hiding things."

I struggled up to her shoulder and rested our foreheads together. "I don't want you to think badly of me. I don't want you to be afraid of what I really am."

"Nothing you could do would make me afraid of you," Zandra said. "You're perfect. A wonderful misfit who surrounds herself with others just like her and shows them how incredible they are. I heard you talking to Sage, telling her she's the perfect familiar for Vorana. You always do that for others, but you need to do it for yourself, too. And you need to do it for us."

I drew in a shaky breath, growing stronger in my witch's embrace. "I am. I will."

"Good. Because if we're not working together now, we'll never get free. And then Gaian and Lila will have won, and we'll either be dead or packing our bags and looking for a new place to live."

"That would be tiresome."

"The dead bit or the packing bit?"

"It's a tie."

Zandra chuckled. "So, what do you say? Shall we join forces, blast the heck out of this attic, kick some gremlin butt, and save our friends?"

I nuzzled Zandra's ear and let out a long, slow breath. "Let's obliterate those devious gremlins once and for all."

Chapter 22

Group magic

We stood in a semicircle facing the attic hatch. I was with Zandra, my paws pressed firmly on her foot. Sammy was next to me, and I was touching him. He trembled beneath my paw, but held fast, a determined look on his fuzzy face. On the opposite side of Zandra stood Vorana and Sage. Sorcha stood next to them, one hand clasping Vorana's. Her other hand rested on Tinkerbell's head. Even that grumpy turncoat was willing to assist in ensuring a successful escape for all of us.

I focused on tapping the magic inside me. Every spell and ability I possessed. This wasn't the time to hold back. My witch's life, my friends, and the town depended on us.

"Is everybody ready?" I asked.

The group nodded, and Zandra rested a hand briefly on my head and scratched her nails through my fur. "You've got this."

"Only with you by my side." My old power shook through me, making my toe beans hot and my fur bristle. The air was charged with magic, thin shimmers of power wafting around us as everyone opened their energies.

"On three," I said. "We focus our release spell on a single point on that hatch. We don't stop until it's dust."

"One, two, three!" Zandra yelled.

Magic poured out of us, filling the attic with rainbow sparkles of energy. It blasted onto the hatch, a laser light beam of intense power that heated the room and sucked away the air. The magic holding us inside groaned and protested, and flickers of black energy snaked around us like toxic vines looking for something to grab and drag away.

"Hold steady, everyone," Vorana said. "It's just trying to scare us."

"This chaos magic is strong." Sammy grunted as he poured more magic into the release spell.

The wood cracked, and a blast of foul-smelling black smoke consumed us, swirling around the group and blinding us with grit and toxic fumes that forced into our mouths and lungs, making us gag.

I dug my front claws into the wooden floor and let out a final blast of energy. There was another crack, the smoke vanished, and the hatch sprung open.

"We did it!" Zandra crouched and kissed my head.

"No time to celebrate. Let's move," I said. "Someone downstairs will have heard the wood splinter, and we can't wait for Gaian or Lila to catch us."

After a quick check around the group to make sure everyone survived, we hurried down the wooden attic stairs. It was quiet in the bedrooms, no sounds coming from any of the rooms.

"Vorana, go with Sage and see if you can get Cythera and Finn free," I said. "We need them to make the arrest." And as backup. Angels were hard to take down in a fight if things got complicated.

Vorana hesitated. "Won't you need us when you confront Gaian and Lila?"

We would, but we also needed powerful angels who weren't concerned about leaping into a fight and handing out justice.

"We'll help," Sammy said. "I know a little about the gremlin magic Gaian has been using. Tinkerbell does, too. We can get Finn and Cythera free."

"We can't trust you," Sage said.

"This is our chance to prove ourselves. Please! We want to do the right thing."

"Speak for yourself," Tinkerbell grumbled.

Sammy nudged her with his head. "Angel Force will go easier on you if you assist."

She sighed. "Fine. Let's see what we can do to get out of this disaster zone."

We crept down the main stairs and separated at the bottom. I remained with Zandra, Sorcha, Vorana, and Sage as we searched for Gaian, Lila, and Ember. I'd put my faith in Sammy to not get tugged back onto a dark path. If he failed, this mission would be impossible to succeed in.

"There are voices coming from Lila's office," Zandra whispered.

We hurried toward the office, slowing when we were within earshot of the conversation.

"It's not too late." Gaian's tone was sharp. "If we act now, there'll be nothing the Court can do. I've got this under control."

"You keep saying that, but why do we have an attic full of prisoners, a trapped ghost, and two dead bodies in the cellar?" Lila's voice was high-pitched, panic snapping each word.

"They're casualties of war. Don't back out now, sister. We're so close to victory I can taste it."

"They're brother and sister?" Sorcha whispered. "I had no idea."

"It makes sense. When I saw them bickering, there was a familiarity to their interaction." I gestured for the others to remain back and then crept to the door, peeking through the small gap. Gaian and Lila were looking at paperwork scattered across Lila's desk. Ember was perched on Gaian's shoulder.

"We can't waste another second. The Gremlin Court has already sent two meddling representatives. When they don't report back soon, they'll send more." Gaian jabbed a finger at the papers. "When we're this close to success, nothing must get in our way."

"They must have had us under surveillance. They don't trust us." Lila scowled at her brother.

"We'll prove they have nothing to worry about," Gaian said. "There's only one more place we need to put the symbols and then the circle of chaos will be complete."

Lila shoved his shoulder. "You shouldn't have gotten rid of the cats. They could have fixed the final symbols for us."

"I couldn't keep forcing chaos magic into them, or they'd have dropped down dead. Besides, I must be the one to complete the circle."

"You mean you want to be seen as the victor. The proud hero the Gremlin Court will celebrate because you captured Crimson Cove. I suppose you're hoping to get a place in court out of this. If you do, you'd better not leave me behind," Lila said.

"Why shouldn't I get a place at the table of power? I've done most of the work while you've tinkered on the edges with this stupid place. If you hadn't taken so long to get things ready, we'd be farther ahead, and the Court wouldn't have sent snoops to interfere."

"Don't blame this on me! You're the one who's been wasting time on that vampire witch. I know you're in love with her."

Gaian snorted. "I needed Sorcha as cover. It was the only way I could infiltrate the town."

I glanced back at Sorcha. Her face was pale, but her expression was determined. She flashed her fangs and slid one finger across her throat.

I nodded. It was time to confront the enemy. I stepped back and blasted the door open with a spell.

Gaian and Lila jumped back from the desk then Gaian scowled. He twisted his hands in the air and slammed a fireball at me.

I ducked the spell, and it was whipped away by Zandra, who was crouched, ready for a fight, magic sparking on her palms. Vorana and Sage also looked battle ready. Sorcha's glare was so scary as she fixed it on Gaian, it even made me flinch.

Gaian stepped forward, crackling with magical energy.

I lunged at him, my murder mittens extended. He dodged out of the way and sent a blast of magic at me, but I ducked it. Lila and Ember spread out, looking for an opening or a weakness to exploit.

I hissed, trying to keep my eyes on all of them.

Ember lunged at Sage. She yowled, dodging his first attack. Then they collided in a frenzy of claws and sparks.

Lila advanced on me, her hands twisting in sinister shapes. A spear of energy shot toward me but fizzled against a shield spell Zandra thrust in front of me.

Gaian's eyes widened in rage. "Kill them!"

I smirked. "Your twisted, borrowed magic can't beat us."

Gaian let out an enraged howl. Lila redoubled her efforts, throwing everything in her arsenal at me, but Zandra's shield held, and the magic bounced away.

Sage shrieked as Ember landed a blow, and fur flew through the air. My heart clenched in concern for my friend, but I didn't dare break my focus. "Sage, get closer to me! Use our shield."

Vorana hurled a blast of multi-colored magic at Ember, making him whimper and retreat behind Gaian's legs.

"Get back out there!" Gaian grabbed at Ember, but he ducked away.

Sage dove under my shield with Vorana. We stood together, power thrumming between us. "Ready?"

Sage nodded, her eyes burning with focused rage. "Ready for some obliteration."

We unleashed our combined power in a rush. The blast sent Gaian and Lila crashing against the wall, and Ember yowled in terror.

Gaian's eyes glowed red with fury as he hurled a crackling bolt of energy at me. I deflected it back at him. He dove aside, the magic scorching the wall behind him.

"Your parlor tricks won't save you forever!" Lila shrieked. She flung out both hands, tendrils of dark power snaking toward me.

I chanted a binding spell, weaving starlight into ropes of magic to ensnare her wrists. Her spell fizzled as I yanked her hands down to her sides. She screamed, struggling against my magic's iron grip.

Sorcha had stayed back from the fight, but now Gaian was wide open, she flew at him, her hands clawed and fangs exposed. She jumped on him and bit his neck.

Ember pounced at Sage again, his jaw opening wide to reveal gleaming, sharp teeth. Sage hissed, her feline form shimmering as she changed into a fiery version of a giant cougar—her body crackling with ethereal flames. She was stunning and terrifying.

Ember raked his claws across Sage's face but was no match for her magnificent new form, and she batted him away with a giant paw.

Gaian hurled spears of black magic at blinding speed. They pierced the shield and our protection shattered.

I twirled, my shimmering coat deflecting each hit as I wove defensive spells to keep Zandra safe. But my energy was waning against the onslaught, and the effort of breaking out of the attic had drained me.

Sage morphed back to her cat form, bleeding from vicious wounds on her side but still hissing defiance at a cowering Ember, who was bloodied from the fight and on his back, his belly exposed as he admitted defeat.

Gaian struggled with Sorcha as they performed a morbid dance of spell-and-fang around the room. He shook her free, but she reared back and landed a disabling blow to his groin with her foot.

"What's going on?" Dimitri appeared in the doorway, shock on his face as he took in the chaos, blood, and magic.

Gaian took advantage of the distraction, shoved Sorcha back, and threw a spell at me. It pinned me against the wall with writhing black chains of power. I struggled in vain against his magic's steely grip, but my strength was gone. I'd used up my magic keeping Zandra safe.

"I'll make you suffer for this insult," Gaian snarled. "And your witch will join you in the torment I have planned. Her vampire freak friend, too. Anyone who gets in our way will wish they hadn't."

Zandra shrieked as Lila's spell hit her, and dark magic coiled around her. I felt her agony and terror through our bond, which fueled my determination to get free, but I needed time to recharge. "Dimitri, do something!"

He stood frozen to the spot, his mouth hanging open. "I... I..."

I closed my eyes, summoning the deepest recesses of my ancient magic. It surged through the earth, filling me with a primal power I hadn't felt in decades. My eyes flew open. I flung out my paws, channeling the magic at Gaian's chest.

A blinding flash lit the room. Gaian and Lila collapsed.

The ancient power left me in a rush. I dropped next to Sage, every part of my body trembling in the aftermath of using so much old power. It should have been beyond me.

"I knew you had it in you," Sage wheezed out.

"You're a true friend. But a bleeding one. How bad is it?"

"I've been worse. But not by much."

"Dimitri! Arrest them." Zandra ran over, grabbed his shoulder, and shook him. "We know who killed Doctor and Mrs. Simister! It was Gaian and Lila."

"And they've been hiding an affiliation to gremlin chaos magic," I said. "The same goes for Ember."

Ember hissed softly from the corner of the room.

Dimitri blinked several times. "Are... are you sure?"

I stared at him. "Yes! Go do your job. Or go get Cythera and Finn. They should be out by now."

Dimitri looked like he was about to pass out. "I'll get help. Cythera will know what to do." He dashed out of the room.

A few seconds later, cool air zoomed over my head, and Lila and Gaian were pinned to the wall by Cythera and Finn. Ember was on the floor, cowering in the corner again, trying to make himself small so the angels wouldn't get him.

Lila screeched, slammed her hands into Finn's chest, and broke free. He caught her around the neck, breaking her necklace as she struggled in his strong grip. It fell to the floor, and Lila convulsed several times before her disguise vanished, and her true gremlin form revealed itself. She was compact, her skin a greenish hue, with large, expressive amber eyes that gleamed with anger. Her teeth were pointed, but her ears were rounded, so she wasn't pure gremlin.

Ember made a break for freedom, speeding to the door, but I shot out a restraining spell that lifted him and placed him on top of a filing cabinet. I stepped forward and sniffed the necklace. It reeked of toxic, foul magic. Not gremlin. Something nastier.

"Nice to have you back with us," I said to Finn.

He flashed me a smile. "Seems you've been busy while we took a break."

"You don't know the half of it." Zandra stood with magic shimmering on her fingertips.

"We've done nothing wrong," Gaian said. "Why are you punishing us?"

Cythera's wings flared behind her. "You're both under arrest for so many crimes I'll run out of breath by listing them all. Remove the magic keeping us trapped in this inn so we can take you to the cells."

Lila made a grab for the necklace on the floor, but Finn held her firmly. She shot a loathsome glare at Gaian. "It's his fault."

"Don't say a word," he snarled. "They've got nothing on us."

"Dark magic spells, two bodies in the cellar, a trapped spirit, and abandoned fluffy recruits willing to tell us what devious plans you've been making suggest otherwise," I said. "But I'm happy to give everyone a summary to get the angels up to speed."

"We'd appreciate that," Finn said. "And then we need food. I'm starving. I even considered eating Cythera."

She tutted. "Don't be ridiculous."

"I'll make this quick, then," I said. "Gaian and Lila are brother and sister. And as you can see by Lila's true form, they have gremlin blood running through their veins. Although not one hundred percent gremlin. Lila, are you also a hobgoblin? Those ears are wonderful. Are those tufts?"

"Gaian's not my brother. He's an idiot with delusions of grandeur," Lila said. "My mother made a huge mistake when she got drunk and bumped into his moron of a father."

"I'm the idiot? You're too stupid to know what the word 'hurry' means," Gaian said. "I kept telling you not to waste time on this place, but you begged for another week and then another. We'd own Crimson Cove by now if it wasn't for you."

"Why did you kill Doctor and Mrs. Simister?" Cythera asked.

"They were sent here to see why the takeover hadn't been achieved," I said.

"They were interfering and doubting our abilities," Lila said. "Just like my parents. They didn't believe in me."

"So, you killed them?" I asked.

Lila huffed out a breath and glanced at Gaian.

"This is a misunderstanding," Gaian said smoothly. "The Simisters weren't killed because they were gremlins. You all know me. I'm about protecting the planet and the people I care about. Sorcha, babe. I love you. You know I'd never do anything shady."

"In case the kick to your groin wasn't clear enough, I don't love you." Sorcha's eyes shimmered with tears, but her head was up and her arms crossed over her chest.

"Babe! Come on! We had fun. I even taught you a few things. We can still be good together."

"You lie to people and pretend to care about them to get what you want," Sorcha said. "Cythera, give me five minutes alone in a room with this idiot. I'll teach him to never disrespect women again."

"As tempting as that is, and I can understand why you're asking, I'll have to refuse your request," Cythera said. "How do we know Doctor and Mrs. Simister were gremlins in disguise?"

"There were clues," I said. "And no one can hide their true nature for long. In their case, the magic surrounding the inn injured Mrs. Simister, and I saw her disguise fail for a few seconds. Their eating habits also suggested they enjoyed feasting gremlin style. And then there were the marks on the wood."

"And on the beam that killed Doctor Simister?" Cythera said.

"Exactly. You just have to figure out whether it was Lila or Gaian who damaged the beam. But I imagine the killer was aiming for either of them. And if I had to pick a name, I'd say it was Lila."

"It wasn't me!" Lila snapped her teeth at Finn.

"I'm not going down for Doctor Simister's murder," Gaian said. "She did it. This is all her doing."

"I thought you said we weren't supposed to say anything?" Lila said. "The second trouble comes our way, you squawk like a baby griffin. He's as guilty as me."

Gaian smirked and turned his attention to Sorcha. "Come to me, my love. This is a misunderstanding. It's time you confessed your crimes. You did all of this, didn't you? The symbols, the murders, the chaos." He moved his fingers in a strange formation, lifting them up and down and twisting them in the air.

"You're out of your mind," Sorcha said. "I'm not protecting you."

Gaian frowned. "I had nothing to do with the killings. Confess! I demand it."

"You can't control Sorcha anymore," I said. "We've removed the chaos symbols you placed on her skin. And we know you drugged her."

Gaian growled. "Sammy, Tinkerbell. Come to me."

There was a faint shuffle behind us, and Sammy and Tinkerbell appeared. I kept watch on Gaian and Lila as I hurried to Sammy's side. "Don't be fooled by his fake charm. I know he's used compulsion magic on you, but you must fight it."

Sammy wheezed out a breath. "I want to. I can't keep doing this, but his magic still lingers inside me."

Tinkerbell grumbled an agreement but made no move toward Gaian.

"You helped us when we were stuck in a deadly situation. What you've been doing is wrong, but your assistance will be looked on favorably when it comes to sentencing. You've been under the influence of toxic, damaging magic. Angel Force won't punish you severely. This wasn't all your fault."

"You're just saying that," Tinkerbell said. "We won't see the outside of a cell for at least a decade."

"I don't care if I'm locked away for good," Sammy said. "I'm sick of being on the wrong side. My life isn't worth living anymore. This is barely an existence. Things have to change."

"And they will." My heart ached to see my former snuggle buddy in such a dark place. "You're surrounded by friends and people who care about you. Even you, Tinkerbell, though I'm not sure you always deserve it."

Sorcha looked down at Tinkerbell. "You're welcome to come back and live with me. I know things were difficult between us, but if we work on it together, we can find a way forward."

Tinkerbell looked stunned by the offer then glanced away. "I'll think about it. I won't go back to that moron, though. Gaian's too much hassle. He can take his weird magic and stuff it."

Gaian snarled. "I don't need either of you! We still have supporters. There are those in Crimson Cove who want this. They welcome the chaos and the darkness."

Dimitri reappeared in the doorway, a mask of confusion on his face. He was sweating. "Oh! Everyone's here."

"Cythera, this is Dimitri. He's been... some help during this crisis." Dimitri trembled, and his wings drooped behind him. He looked terrified of something.

"Where have you been?" Cythera snapped. "You should have been protecting civilians."

"I thought I'd try to find a way for us to get out, but the magic is holding. Are you certain you have the right people?"

"We've found our killers." Cythera's gaze moved over him, and a disapproving look crossed her face.

I looked up at Dimitri as he shuffled his feet and tugged at his collar. Then I turned my attention to Ember, who was still on the filing cabinet. "I've not been able to figure out why you became involved with Gaian and Lila."

He squirmed in the spell I held him in then stilled. "The great Juno doesn't have it all worked out in that genius mind of yours? You're not so impressive after all."

"I'm impressive enough. But you're a mystery, brought in by Sage, so I don't know your background."

"Let me go, and I'll tell you everything."

"You're staying here," I said. "You're captured either way, so it makes no difference to me if you share your secrets. But I'm curious about you. You could have had everything. A wonderful witch to bond with, education, family, yet you chose the gremlin way of life. You favor chaos over calm."

Ember didn't speak.

"We raised Ember after he was dumped," Lila said. "He reminded me of Gaian and me. We got kicked out of our homes when our mothers' indiscretions were discovered. Ember was also abandoned. We found him when he was young, starving in the woods. We adopted him. I had no idea we'd gotten ourselves such a powerful creature."

"And one with serious anger issues," Gaian said. "I've lost count of the number of times that thing bit me."

"Because you didn't always treat him kindly," Lila said. "When Ember got an invitation to come to Crimson Cove and join with a witch, we knew luck was on our side, so we acted."

"I never fitted in anywhere," Ember said on a huff. "I was always told I was odd, so I knew I'd never find a true familiar bond. I tried a couple of times, but the witches rejected me. I wanted more out of life, so I stuck with what I knew, especially when I learned about Gaian and Lila's plans to take over this place."

"I knew you couldn't be trusted," Sage said.

"Ember, you didn't have to lie to me about what you were doing here," Vorana said. "I'd have taken you in and cared for you. And there's nothing wrong with you. You're perfect. It's just that you've gotten on the wrong path. You can change if you want to. I can help you. Sage will, too."

Sage grumbled under her breath. "I suppose we all make mistakes."

Ember hiccupped, taking his time as he inspected his paws. "It's too late for me. No one loves me. Lila and Gaian only kept me around because of what I could do for them. Forget about me."

My heart went out to the tortured little cat, but I couldn't forgive him for the damage he'd done to our town.

"So, we have our killers," Cythera said, "and their accomplices. It's time to figure out how to get out of here."

"Not just yet," I said. "There's one more accomplice who hasn't stepped forward. Isn't that right, Dimitri?"

Chapter 23

Final feather

Dimitri took a step back, his wings fluttering behind him. "Me? I'm not involved with what's going on. I've been helping. I'm on your side."

"I've barely had time to think about how unusual it was that you got in when we all failed to get out," I said. "You couldn't have come down the chimney without the gremlins' permission."

"I did! I told you, I worked with other angels. We were powerful enough to break through the barrier. Not by much, but it was enough for me to get in."

I shook my head. "We used every spell we had, and none of them made a dent in the power surrounding this inn."

"And you never will," Gaian said. "Chaos symbols surround this place, and you'll find them in every room and under every floor. If you want to get out, the chaos magic will make sure you fail. It loves to feel defeat. It thrives on it."

"You're using more than chaos magic," I said. "That necklace Lila was wearing stinks of darkness.

You've gotten in over your heads, but you're not willing to accept it."

Gaian shrugged. "I used what was necessary to achieve the right results. And I'd do it again. But I'd have less baggage next time." He glared at Lila.

I focused back on Dimitri. "You didn't get help from any angels to break in. And you wouldn't have been able to fly to Crimson Cove to help, given the crazy weather."

Dimitri gulped. "Maybe we walked in or took the bus."

"Zandra, you and Vorana look after Gaian," Cythera said. "I need to check something with Dimitri."

"Let me." Sorcha flashed her fangs. "We have unfinished business."

"You stay there." Cythera pointed at Sorcha. "Unless you want to be arrested, too."

Sorcha scowled then nodded.

"Be careful," I said to Zandra as she hurried over with Vorana.

Cythera joined me, and her gaze flicked up and down Dimitri several times. "I don't know you."

"I'm fresh out of training. I'm glad you're free. This has been a wild first case to handle on my own." Dimitri inched back. "Should I try getting out again?"

Cythera flared her nostrils. "Juno is right about you. You have the wrong uniform lapels, and those boots are non-standard issue."

"I got dressed in a hurry." Dimitri stared down at his boots. "None of us had time to think when we heard what was going on here. We acted for the good of the town. You can't reprimand me for grabbing the wrong boots!"

Cythera shook her head. "No matter how desperate the situation, Angel Force would never send a new graduate into such dangerous conditions. We're a responsible employer."

He gestured at a window. "You don't know what it's like out there. We had to try anything. They needed a volunteer, so I stepped up."

"The gremlins sent you in as a spy to assess the situation," I said. "And you were keen for us to focus on Willow as the killer. You also weren't interested in other clues I pointed out."

"I was! I keep saying I was helping." Sweat trickled down the side of Dimitri's face.

"You weren't interested that Lila took Doctor Simister's briefcase containing the Crimson Cove file. You deflected me from that." I narrowed my eyes. "I'm assuming one of your parents was a gremlin, too? Are you also Gaian and Lila's sibling?"

He scowled at me, and a green shimmer flashed across his wings.

"Answer the cat," Cythera said. "I'll be able to check your credentials as soon as I'm out of here. Then I'll know you're lying. Impersonating a member of law enforcement carries a fine and ten years in prison."

Dimitri's shoulders slumped. "So what if our father was a player when he was younger? He cares for us, and we're his army of willing recruits. An advance guard to set his plans into motion."

"His plan being to take over Crimson Cove?" I asked.

"And then some," Lila said. "The trouble was he kept getting distracted by a pretty face. I don't know how many half-brothers and sisters I've got out there. Dimitri and Gaian are just two of them, the useless lumps of dirt."

"Dad always knew what he was doing," Gaian said. "You just don't like it because he prefers me over you."

"He doesn't care about any of us, not really," Lila said. "That's why I want to prove myself to him. If we'd taken over Crimson Cove, he'd have noticed me. He'd have given me the respect I deserve. Instead, the last time I saw him, he introduced me to one of his disgusting friends, the one with the wart on his nose and ear tufts, and said I was suitable as marriage material but not much else."

"So, you wanted to show your father you had value to him," I said. "And in doing so, you almost destroyed our wonderful town."

"It would have been worth it," Dimitri said. "And you won't stop us for long. We'll escape or get out. There's nothing you can do."

Cythera whacked Dimitri on the head with her wing, and he crashed to the floor. "Can't we?"

***

Just over twenty-four hours had passed since the conspiracy to take over Crimson Cove had been uncovered and the killers and their accomplices caught.

Dawn was breaking over a new morning, and I was with Zandra, Finn, and Cythera, along with nearly all the town's residents, most of whom carried buckets of magic and scrubbing brushes as we hunted for the last of the gremlin chaos symbols and removed them.

We'd broken out of the inn after discovering and scouring away over twenty sets of chaos symbols. After that, it had been a busy night, and we hadn't taken a proper break since taking Gaian, Lila, Dimitri, Ember, Tinkerbell, and Sammy to the Angel Force cells.

Finn set down his empty bucket of magic and leaned against the wall. Just like the rest of us, he wore a cloak of exhaustion, but there was a smile on his face as he looked around. "It's shaping up to be a nice day."

I squinted at the rising sun. "It feels like a day for sleeping in, several large breakfasts, and then hanging out with my favorite people." I leaned against Zandra's leg.

"That works for me," she said. She raised a hand as Vorana, Sage, and Sorcha walked over to join us. "How are you getting on with your cleanup?"

"All done," Vorana said. "A crew is checking a street in the East quadrant, then we should be ready to pack up. We got rid of over a thousand symbols."

"Same here," Finn said. "Those gremlins sure were sneaky."

"And they weren't working alone." Cythera had her back to us as she scanned the street. "The Gremlin Court has been making power plays for months. To begin with, we thought it was a baseless rumor, but I've been doing some digging, and there have been a number of attempted coups in prime magical hotspots. No one is happy about it. They've gone after an ancient vampire hive, a mermaid mount, and a town full of powerful banshees."

"What's got the gremlins so riled that they're making these sneaky assaults on power bases?" I asked.

"They do this from time to time. Check the historical records, and you'll find the gremlins rise up for the joy of creating instability."

"They feed off it," Vorana said. "It's their mojo."

"The magic community is furious. We're united against the Gremlin Court, and reparations will be made." Cythera checked her watch and tutted. "They won't get away with it."

"How are you doing?" Zandra asked Sorcha.

"I feel like an idiot," Sorcha said. "Gaian had me convinced he was the perfect guy. And I can't believe he's ruined my café."

"It's not your fault." Vorana placed an arm around Sorcha's shoulders. "Gaian used you to get what he wanted. It sounds like he's been drugging you and using those gremlin symbols against you the whole time you were together."

"It was no wonder your mind got scrambled," Zandra said.

"I should have known something was off. You two could have told me," Sorcha said.

Zandra raised a hand. "Hey, this isn't our fault. We tried to warn you about him, but you shut us out."

Sorcha sighed. "Yeah, sorry. I'm angry with myself, not you. I got sucked into his web of lies, and I abandoned everything I love. I stopped caring about the café, the vampires, the waifs and strays in town. I don't know how many people I've hurt."

"You're already making amends," I said. "Not that you have to. I heard you're planning an all-nighter for the vampires to say sorry with free food and drink."

"It's the least I can do," Sorcha said.

"And you've been speaking to me to see if I need help at the sanctuary," Finn said. "I've got three troubled, hissing, clawed fluffies coming your way tomorrow."

"They'll be welcome." Sorcha shook her head. "I wish I'd never met Gaian. I feel responsible for all of this."

"Don't. If Gaian hadn't met you when you were on that retreat, he'd have found another way to sneak into Crimson Cove," I said. "We couldn't have stopped this."

"But we did," Finn said. "Gaian and Lila will be charged with murder, and Ember and Dimitri have confessed that they were accomplices. They'll serve time for their crimes."

"What about Sammy and Tinkerbell?" My heart gave a worried thump at the thought of my former snuggle buddy behind bars.

Finn's expression turned mournful. "They're up to their ear tips in this. And not just for being accomplices in attempting to take over Crimson Cove. They're also wanted for crimes relating to the demon who infiltrated the town and tried to take our magic."

"I want to defend Sammy," I said. "A powerful werewolf potion damaged him when he was helping me with another case. If I'd known it was causing him trouble, none of this would have happened."

"That'll be taken into account," Finn said. "The same goes for Tinkerbell. We know she's had a rough past and got herself messed up with the wrong crowd a few times, and they helped us to break out of the inn once we'd captured Gaian and Lila."

"And they set you and Cythera free from that room. They didn't have to do that."

"There'll be leniency when their cases are reviewed," Cythera said. "But we can't allow them to get away with causing so many problems. It'll send the wrong signal."

My heart sank. "I'd like to see Sammy."

"And I'd like to see Tinkerbell," Sorcha said. "We have bridges to rebuild, but I'm hopeful she'll want to come back and live with me."

"Once she's served her sentence, she'll need somewhere stable to stay," Cythera said. "But there'll be a lengthy period of rehabilitation for both of them."

"We can visit them now, though?" I asked. "They're still in town?"

"They're going through some hefty magical detox," Finn said. "It'll be a few days before you can see them. I'll get you in as soon as possible."

"I'd appreciate that. I have a lot of making up to do with Sammy." I was full of regrets that I'd missed the signs he was struggling. I was uncertain if we'd ever get back to what we once were, but I considered him a friend, and I'd do whatever I needed to, to make sure he was happy again.

Cythera tapped her foot on the ground.

"Is something troubling you?" I asked.

"There he is." Cythera strode away as a ridiculously handsome angel with a lion's mane of blond hair landed in the dirt and caught hold of her hand. He bowed and kissed the back of it.

"My dearest Cythera. A thousand apologies for being late."

"You know I can't stand tardiness. It's bad manners. Let's move."

"Wait! Who is this?" I hurried after them. "Aren't you going to introduce me to your friend?"

The supermodel-handsome angel dropped Cythera's hand and turned to me. "It's always a pleasure to meet one of my fiancée's friends. And you are..."

"That cat is not my friend," Cythera said. "We need to hurry, or I'll miss the appointment. I've already had to reschedule it once, thanks to some irksome gremlins."

"Of course, my love. I was delighted when you asked me to accompany you to your dress fitting."

"Fiancée? You're engaged to Cythera?" I looked over my shoulder to see the others were equally stunned. Finn's jaw was almost on the ground.

"I'm sure Cythera must have mentioned me. I'm Metatron Silverio St. Clair. My friends call me Maverick." He winked at me. "I was fortunate the charming Cythera accepted my proposal a month ago. I've been blissfully happy ever since as we've discussed wedding plans, where we'll live, and our future family."

"Stop talking and move." Cythera's cheeks were flushed a dull red, and she wouldn't meet my eye.

"As you wish, my dearest." Maverick bowed to all of us. "I expect I'll see a lot more of you. And I hope you can all make the wedding." He strode away, clasping Cythera's hand and insisting she hold it.

"We wouldn't miss it." I turned back to the others. "What just happened?"

Finn snort laughed. "Cythera's getting married?"

"I never thought I'd see the day," Vorana said. "She's so fiercely independent. I've not seen her go on a date in years, and now she's marrying a hot guy from an eighties hunk fest movie. And what a hunk!" She fanned her face with a hand.

"That must be what's making her so grumpy," Sorcha said. "And I know how she feels. I'm staying clear of men. I'm having 'single and happy' tattooed across my forehead and barring all male creatures from the café."

Finn stared after Cythera, still smiling. "I hope you don't consider me male enough to be excluded."

Sorcha twisted her mouth to the side. "I'll make an exception for you. But no flirting."

I stood with my friends as they gossiped over Cythera's shocking engagement. My gaze went along the street to where small groups of residents walked, buckets of magic in hand as they worked together to ensure the town was safe once again.

I waved at Adrienne and her boyfriend, Joel. They were back to their normal, non-bitey ghoulish selves. They were accompanied by Cannibal Bill, who'd survived their feasting intentions.

Zandra crouched beside me. "Haven't you got something to do?"

"I have. Be back in a moment." I trotted a short distance to the Whispering Willow inn. To look at it, you'd never know what murderous chaos had gone on. The air was still and warm, the birds were just beginning to sing, and the building looked inviting.

I headed inside and down to the cellar. Willow was still there, trapped inside the pot. I'd taken an hour off of symbol hunting to read through an old hex book in Zandra's chest of magic, and when I'd been helping rid the inn of the chaos symbols, I'd found just the thing to help a ghost in need.

It only took a second to break the magic keeping her inside the pot. Willow rushed out in a chilly swirl and zoomed around the cellar.

"Be calm! You're free. And no one will hurt you." I stood in the center of the room, tracing lines of power with my paw as I waited for her to settle.

Willow slowed, her form becoming the familiar shape of a sad-eyed young woman. "You came back for me!"

"I told you I'd help. Sorry it took so long. We had gremlin mischief to deal with."

"Gremlins!"

"You really didn't know what they were planning?" I finished the last line in my power spell.

"No! All this time, it was gremlins." She shook her head. "Lila?"

"A gremlin-hobgoblin, looking to impress her father."

"Oh! Anyone else?"

"Several more. But I'm here to set you free, not gossip. If you're ready."

Willow licked her lips. "You really can help set me free?"

"I wasn't certain, but then I found this." I dragged a crumbling, filthy poppet from a shelf and placed it in the center of my spell. "If I'm not mistaken, the poppet's hair once belonged to you."

She drew in a ragged breath, her gaze glued to the crude poppet doll. "That's how he caught me?"

I nodded. "We learned what a powerful weather witch you were, so I was surprised anyone could have trapped you. I knew then that it had to be an object keeping you here. Something personal to you. When I was hunting for chaos symbols, I discovered the poppet under a floorboard."

Willow's eyes grew hazy. "He must have stolen my hairbrush. I had a room here, so it would have been easy for him to get it."

"I destroy the poppet, and you can leave."

Willow's gaze lifted to the stairs. Zandra stood there, a smile on her face as she gestured for me to continue.

"Say the word, and you'll get your freedom," I said to Willow.

"I've been ready for hundreds of years. I have so much to see and do. But first, I plan to stay somewhere modern, with high ceilings, air conditioning, and a cellar that doesn't stink of vermin."

"There are new apartments on the other side of town," Zandra said. "The residents would enjoy a good old-fashioned haunting."

I chuckled. "That sounds like fun."

Willow giggled then her smile faded. "Thank you, Juno. I'll be forever in your debt. Anytime you need a friend, you just call."

"It's been a pleasure." I stepped on the poppet, and it burst into flames.

Willow squeaked then a joyful laugh flew from her mouth as she swirled around the cellar, pressed a kiss to my head, and vanished through the coal chute.

Zandra walked down the rest of the steps. She reached down and lifted me onto her shoulder before stamping out the tiny flames and crushing the remains of the poppet under her boot. "You figured things out again."

"With your help. With everyone's help."

She arched an eyebrow. "And with a little of your extra magic."

I exhaled slowly. "All of it. I held nothing back."

"Yeah. I know. It was epic."

My gut clenched. "And..."

"And scary. But I'm not scared off. You'll never scare me away. I love you, Juno."

I tugged on a piece of itchy fur, and a chunk came away in my mouth. I spat it out and stared at it as it floated to the floor. "Even if I become a furless, tailless mess, who spurts out odd magic all over the place?"

"Especially then. You're my misfit, and you're perfect for me."

I purred softly and leaned against her ear. "And you're mine. I love you, too."

"Shall we go get bacon and sausage sandwiches at the café? Sorcha's buying."

"That's an offer I can't refuse. Maybe I'll add a few slices of smoked salmon, too. I've missed my salmon."

As we headed out of the inn and re-joined the others, the sun lifted higher, bathing us in a warm glow as we walked along the street, greeting friends and reassuring everyone Crimson Cove was safe.

For now.

About the Author

K.E. O'Connor (Karen) is a mystery author living in the beautiful British countryside. She loves all things mystery, animals, and cake.

If you want to practice spells, solve a few murders, and spend time with amazing witches and their talking familiars, join her weekly newsletter.

Sign up today.
Newsletter: https://BookHip.com/GXDVFRA
Website: www.keoconnor.com/writing
Facebook: www.facebook.com/keoconnorauthor

Also By

Witch Haven: Welcome to Witch Haven, where nothing is what it seems. Meet four fabulous witches as they struggle with their destinies, deal with misfiring magic, murder, and the Magic Council.

Crypt Witches: Meet Tempest Crypt, a witch who swallows demons, and Wiggles, her mini talking hellhound, while you enjoy magical murder and intrigue.

Lorna Shadow: A cozy mystery series set in the fun world of a personal assistant who sees ghosts. Meet Lorna, her ditzy sidekick, Helen, and Flipper, the dog who senses ghosts, as they solve crimes and save the day.

Holly Holmes: An adorable cozy culinary mystery series set in the beautiful village of Audley St. Mary. Each book is full of treats, murder, and twists. Join Holly and Meatball, her clue-hunting dog, as they solve murders and eat cake.